DOCTOR SALLY

The impact of Dr. Sally Smith on the mind of the average male was one of awed reverence. She knew it, but saw no reason to subscribe to the popular belief that a lady doctor must look like a gargoyle with steel-rimmed spectacles and a wash-leather complexion.

But Sally was always strictly professional. She had no time for men—except at the end of a stethoscope—and was particularly censorious of idle young men like Bill Bannister, whose predisposition to fall in love with every pretty girl was the talk of the county.

Forsaking all others, Bill fell for Sally hook, line and sinker. Yet Sally appeared deaf to his wooing—especially when the brassy Lottie Higginbotham bounced upon the scene all set to give her celebrated " woman scorned " act.

" Mr. Wodehouse," said *The Field*, " is the best of doctors, the best of tonics." Only Bill Bannister is likely to quarrel with this verdict and his interest in doctors was essentially biased.

Books by P. G. Wodehouse

DOCTOR SALLY

By

P. G. WODEHOUSE

BARRIE & JENKINS
COMMUNICA · EUROPA

© P. G. Wodehouse 1932

First published in 1952 by
Herbert Jenkins Ltd

This edition published in 1978 by
Barrie and Jenkins Ltd
24 Highbury Crescent London N5 1RX

ISBN 0 257 65763 0

Printed and bound in Great Britain by
REDWOOD BURN LIMITED
Trowbridge & Esher

DOCTOR SALLY

CHAPTER I

THE eighteenth hole at Bingley-on-Sea, that golfers' Mecca on the south coast of England, is one of those freak holes—a very short mashie-shot up a very steep hill off a tee screened from the club-house by a belt of trees. From the terrace, where the stout man in the vivid plus-fours stood waiting for his partner to arrive for the morning round, only the green was visible.

On this green, falling from the sky in a perfect arc, there suddenly descended a white ball. It struck the ground, took a back spin, and rolled to within a foot of the hole.

The stout man congealed like one who has seen a vision. So might a knight of the Middle Ages have looked on beholding the Holy Grail. He had been at Bingley only two days, and so had played this hole only six times, but he knew that if he played it for the rest of his life he would never get a two on it, as this unseen expert was so obviously about to do. Four was Sir Hugo Drake's best—his worst twenty-seven, on the occasion when he overran the green and got imbedded in a sort of Sahara which lay beyond it.

A player like this, he decided, demanded inspection at close range. Possibly it was the pro. taking a little practice, but even the pro. might reasonably expect homage after such a shot. Sir Hugo toddled over to the green, and, having reached it and peered into the depths, stood stunned with amazement.

It was not the pro. It was not a man at all. It was a girl—and a small girl, at that. That she was also extremely pretty seemed of slight importance to

7

Sir Hugo. He was not a man who paid much attention to women's looks. What mattered to him was that he stood in the presence of a female who could handle a mashie like that. And, being a man who liked to give credit where credit was due, he said so.

" My dear young lady," puffed Sir Hugo, " that was an extraordinary fine stroke."

There is a camaraderie among golfers. Girls of the species, complimented on their game by unintroduced males, do not draw themselves up haughtily and say " Sir!" This one smiled. She had a charming smile.

" Where on earth did you learn to play like that?" asked Sir Hugo reverently.

" At Garden City, mostly."

The name was new to Sir Hugo.

" Garden City?"

" It's outside New York."

" Oh?" Sir Hugo was enlightened. He had a deep respect for transatlantic golf. " You come from America?"

" Yes, I've been in London about two years. I'm surprised my game hasn't gone off more. I don't get much time for playing."

Sir Hugo sighed.

" Nor do I," he replied sadly. " A busy specialist, you know. . . . They keep one's nose pretty tightly to the grindstone."

" A specialist?" The girl seemed suddenly interested. " What sort of specialist?"

" Nerves."

" Really?"

" Drake's my name—Sir Hugo Drake."

The girl's interest was now unmistakable. She beamed.

" Fancy!" she said. " I thought your last book

8

was wonderful. This is a proud moment for a mere general practitioner, Sir Hugo."

" A what?"

" A general practitioner. I'm one."

Sir Hugo gaped.

" Good God! You're not a doctor?"

" Yes, I am. Smith—Sally Smith. Doctor Sally Smith."

" Good God!" exclaimed Sir Hugo again.

The suspicion of a shadow passed over the girl's face. She was always meeting men who exclaimed " Good God!" or its equivalent, when informed of her profession, and she disliked it. It seemed to her that they said it in the voice a small boy would use on being introduced to a circus freak. The male mind did not appear to be able to grasp immediately the fact that a woman doctor need not of necessity be a gargoyle with steel-rimmed spectacles and a wash-leather complexion.

However, this was a nice old man, so she decided not to bite his head off.

" I suppose it does seem funny," she said. " But there it is."

" Funny?" said Sir Hugo, recovering. " Not at all. Certainly not. Quite the contrary."

" I like being a doctor, and it doesn't do anybody any harm—at least, I've never killed a patient yet— so what I say to myself is, ' Why not?' "

" Quite," said Sir Hugo. " Why not? Precisely. Very sensible."

The girl tapped her ball into the hole and picked it up.

" Nice course, this," she said.

" Very," said Sir Hugo. " Are you making a long stay?"

"Just a two weeks' vacation. Are you here for long?"

Sir Hugo Drake had now come to look upon this girl as a soul-mate. A member of his own profession and a golfer capable of a two on the eighteenth, she deserved, he felt, his full confidence. He was not a man who, as a rule, discussed his private affairs with strangers, but he could not bring himself to regard as a stranger a girl so outstanding at the short mashie-shot.

"I don't know how long I'm going to be here," he confided. "The fact is, I'm looking for my nephew."

"Have you lost him?" Sally asked, surprised.

"He's given me the slip," said Sir Hugo, turning a deeper mauve, for the affair had caused him much annoyance. "He was living quietly in the country down in Hampshire, and he came up to London, and suddenly he disappeared from London, and I met a man who said he had seen him down here—in company," said Sir Hugo, lowering his voice to a portentous whisper, "with a female of flashy appearance."

Sally smiled.

"Not me," she said.

"I wish it had been you," said Sir Hugo devoutly. "If he would only have the sense to fall in love with a nice girl like you I could be easier in my mind."

"You shouldn't worry."

"But I do worry," said Sir Hugo vehemently. "His poor mother was my sister, and since her death I have regarded myself as *in loco parentis* to the boy. Causes me a great deal of anxiety. Too much money, that's what he's got, and too much time on his hands. When he was at Cambridge he came within an ace," said Sir Hugo, fixing his companion with a gaze calculated to make the flesh creep, "of marrying a girl in a tobacco shop!"

"Boys will be boys."

"Not while I'm *in loco parentis* to them, they won't," said Sir Hugo stoutly. "The trouble with William is that he's impulsive. Got a habit of falling in love at first sight. I don't know who this flashy female is, but I've come down here to break the thing up and take him back to Woollam Chersey, where he belongs."

"Is that the name of his place in the country?"

"Yes."

"I should have thought he would be safe, living in the country."

"He is. He is safe while living in the country. But he keeps dashing away from the country and losing his head. Oh, well, I mustn't bother you with my troubles. I see my partner looking for me."

He whooped and waved his hand at the terrace. A long, thin man, clad, like himself, in plus-fours of a regrettable pattern, whooped and waved back.

"Hope we shall meet again," he said.

"I hope so," said Sally.

"Give me a lesson, perhaps?"

"I should be delighted."

"Good!" said Sir Hugo, and strode off to the first tee.

CHAPTER II

ON the Front—or Esplanade—of Bingley-on-Sea stands the Hotel Superba; and at twenty minutes past four the thin mist which had been hanging over the resort since lunch-time disappeared and there filtered through the windows of suite number seven on the second floor that curious faint gamboge light which passes for sunshine in England. Its mild rays shone deprecatingly on one of those many-coloured carpets peculiar to suites at south coast hotels, on the engraving of "The Stag at Bay" over the mantelpiece, on the table set for tea, and on Marie, maid to Mrs. Higginbotham, who had just deposited on the table a plate of sandwiches.

In addition to the sunshine, there entered also the strains of a dance band, presumably from the winter garden below, where Swiss waiters prowled among potted palms and such of the Superba's guests as wished to do so were encouraged to dance. Carried away by the melody, Marie went so far as to dance a step or two herself. And so absorbed was she in this pursuit that a knocking on the outer door did not penetrate to her consciousness.

It got through, however, to Mrs. Higginbotham in the bedroom, and she gave tongue.

"Marie!"

The maid ceased to pirouette. Her employer's voice was one of those which impress themselves on the most preoccupied.

"Yes, moddom?"

"Are you deaf, you poor fish? Somebody at the door."

" Very good, moddom."

Marie opened the door. There was nothing much to reward her for the effort. Merely a man in spats.

" Mrs. Higginbotham in?" asked this individual.

" Yes, sir."

The visitor crossed the threshold. He was an immaculate and yet somehow subtly battered person in the early thirties. He wore a suit of grey material and unimpeachable cut and—until he removed it— a white bowler hat. In his right eye there was a monocle, and through this he inspected the tea-table. With a slight diminution of what appeared to be a constitutional gloom, he moved towards it and picked up a sandwich.

Mrs. Higginbotham, still a disembodied voice, continued to interest herself in the proceedings.

" Is that you, Bill?"

" It is not Mr. Bannister, moddom. It is——"

Marie looked at the feaster inquiringly. He was now well into his second sandwich, but he could still speak, and did so.

" Lord Tidmouth."

" Who the dickens is Lord Tidmouth?"

The new-comer seemed to feel that he ought to enter into the spirit of this long-distance conversation. He approached the bedroom door.

" What-ho within there! Is that Lottie?"

" Who are you?"

" Tidmouth's the name at the present. It was Bixby till I hooked the old title. I don't know if you remember me. We used to be married once."

Evidently Mrs. Higginbotham possessed one of those highly trained memories from which no fact, however trivial, escapes. She uttered a pleased screech.

" Squiffy!"

" That's right."

" Well, I'm blowed! Where did you spring from?"

" Oh, various parts. I've been travelling a lot. Not been in England for some years. I happened to blow down here and saw you going up in the lift— yesterday, that was—and I asked your name, and they told me you were staying here, so at the earliest opportunity up I popped."

" Splendid! I'll be out in a minute."

" Right-ho. I say, when did you acquire the Higginbotham?"

" About two years ago."

" Is he here?"

" No. Kensal Green Cemetery."

" Oh, well, see you soon."

Lord Tidmouth wandered back to the table and started on another sandwich.

" I shan't be long now," Mrs. Higginbotham assured him. " I'm just shaving."

" What!"

" My neck, you silly ass!"

" Oh!"

" Have a sandwich."

" I am."

" You're what?"

" A sandwich. I mean, I'm having one; and most extraordinarily good they are. Sardine, or my trained senses deceive me."

He tested this theory by taking another, and all doubts were removed.

" Yes," he continued, " absolutely sardine. Lottie!"

" Hullo?"

" I read an interesting thing in the paper the other day," said Lord Tidmouth. " It appears that the sardine's worst enemy is the halibut, and I give you my word that until I read it I didn't know the sardine *had* an enemy. And I don't mind telling you that my opinion of the halibut has gone down considerably. Very considerably. Fancy anything wanting to bully a sardine. I mean to say——"

He would have proceeded further, but at this moment there was a flash of light in the doorway of the bedroom, and he found himself blinking at one of the most vivid suits of pyjamas ever conceived by the diseased mind of a fashionable haberdasher.

"Holy smoke!" he exclaimed. "I mean—well, well, well!"

"Well, well, well!" said Lottie.

"Well, well, well, *well!*" said Lord Tidmouth.

He took her hand in a sort of trance. He was visibly affected. The thought that he had been married to this and had allowed it to get away from him was evidently moving him powerfully. His monocle slipped from his eye and danced madly on the end of its string.

"My Gosh!" he said. "Is that how you look?"

"That's how."

"Well, well, well, well, well, WELL!" said Lord Tidmouth.

Lottie moved to the mirror and scrutinized herself in it. She was pleased that her very considerable beauty had won this striking tribute.

"Sit down," she said.

Lord Tidmouth sat down.

"Tell me all," he said.

"All what?"

"All about yourself. Who was the recent Higginbotham?"

"Oh, a man. Very rich. From up North. I met him when I was in 'Follow the Girl'. I went back to the stage after you and I parted brass-rags. He passed on last July.''

'' Marry again?''

'' Ass! If I had, would my name still be Higginbotham?''

'' Something in that,'' agreed his lordship.

'' I mean, a girl doesn't call herself Higginbotham unless she has to.''

'' Absolutely not.''

'' Still I *am* sort of engaged.''

'' Oh?''

'' To a man named Bannister—Bill Bannister. Country squire sort of chap. Has a big place in Hampshire. Woollam Chersey it's called.''

'' What!'' Lord Tidmouth's manner became almost animated. '' Bill Bannister? One of my oldest pals. I'd like to see old Bill again.''

'' Well, you will, if you stick around. He's calling soon to take me to dance. Tell me about yourself.''

'' Oh, I've just been mooching round.''

'' Did *you* marry again?''

'' Oh, yes, here and there. My second wife ran away with a Frenchman.''

'' Did you get a divorce?''

'' Yes, and married again. My third wife ran away with a Spaniard.''

'' Too bad.''

'' When I married my fourth wife——''

'' Who did she run away with?''

'' A Brazilian.''

'' Your home during the last few years seems to have been a sort of meeting-place of the nations.''

'' Yes.''

'' How many wives have you got now?''

'' None at the moment. The supply has sort of

16

petered out. By the way, talking of wives, how do you feel on the subject of rocking-horses?"

"What on earth are you talking about?"

"You see, to-morrow is my second wife's first son's third birthday, and I've just bought him a rocking-horse."

"You still keep up with them, then?"

"Oh, a fellow has to be civil. Anyway, I've just bought this rocking-horse, and I told the man to send it round here till my train went. You don't mind?"

"Of course not."

"Thanks!"

There was a pause. The jazz band below had now begun to play a waltz of a singularly glutinous nature. Its effect on the pair in the sitting-room seemed to be to induce a certain sentimentality.

"Odd," said Lord Tidmouth.

"What's odd?"

"Meeting again like this after all these years."

"Yes."

There was another pause.

"Dancing much these days?" asked Lord Tidmouth.

"Quite a lot."

"Why not a spot now? Music and everything."

"That's an idea."

They started to dance, and Lord Tidmouth's emotion appeared to deepen. He sighed once or twice.

"Good tune."

"Topping."

Into the rather fish-like eyes of Lord Tidmouth there had begun to creep a strange light, indicative of a brain at work. He was not a man who often thought, but he was thinking now. And what he was thinking was that, conditions having placed such an action within

17

the sphere of practical politics, it would be silly not to kiss this girl. Here she was, he meant to say, within range, as it were, and—well, to put it in a nutshell, what, what?

He kissed her.

And as he did so the door opened and there appeared on the threshold a large young man in a flannel suit. His agreeable face, at the moment of his entry, had been wearing a rather preoccupied look. This, as he observed the entwined couple before him, changed to one of disapproval. He eyed them in silence for a space, then in a cold voice he said:

"Good afternoon!"

The effect of these words on the tender scene was immediate. It broke it up like a bomb. Lord Tidmouth released his erstwhile helpmate and straightened his tie. Lottie bit her tongue.

There was one of those embarrassing pauses.

"I didn't hear you come in," said Lottie.

"So I imagined," said Bill Bannister.

Silence fell again. It was not one of those episodes about which there is much to be said. It impeded rather than inspired conversation.

"Well, I'll go and get dressed," said Lottie.

"I should," said Bill.

Lord Tidmouth, during these exchanges, had been directing at his long-lost friend a look in which remorse and brotherly love were nicely blended. Remorse now faded, and brotherly love had the field to itself. Bill, turning to deal with this cuckoo in the nest, was surprised to observe him advancing with outstretched hand.

"Bill, old man!" said Lord Tidmouth emotionally.

"Eh?" said Bill, at a loss.

Lord Tidmouth sighed.

18

"Have you really forgotten me, Bill?" he said sadly. "Your ancient pal? Well, well, well! Name of Tidmouth. Used to be Bixby."

Bill stared.

"It isn't Squiffy?"

"It *is* Squiffy!"

"For heaven's sake!"

Complete amiability appeared to reign in young Mr. Bannister's bosom once more. He gripped the outstretched hand warmly.

"Well, I'm dashed!"

"Me, too, old boy."

"I haven't seen you for years."

"I haven't seen *you* for years."

They talked for a while of the dear old days, as friends reunited will do.

"I hear you're still living at the old address, Bill," said Lord Tidmouth. "If I hadn't run into you like this I was going to have dropped you a line."

"Why not come down there for a bit?" said Bill hospitably.

Lord Tidmouth looked doubtful.

"Well, I'd love to, Bill, old man," he said; "but the fact is—been having domestic troubles of late, and all that—left me a bit on the moody side. I'm more or less a broken man these days, and don't feel quite up to country-house parties."

"It won't be a country-house party. Just you and me and my uncle."

"Which uncle is that?"

"I've only one—Sir Hugo Drake, the nerve specialist."

"I never met him. Nice chap?"

"Oh, not so bad. He'd be all right if he could get it into his head that I'm a grown-up man and not still a kid in knickerbockers. He will fuss over me like a hen, and it drives me crazy. He has a fit every time I look at a girl. He'd die if he ever saw Lottie."

Lord Tidmouth's manner betrayed a certain embarrassment.

"I say, Bill, old man."

"Hullo?"

Lord Tidmouth coughed.

"Touching on that little contretemps, if I may so express it, which occurred just now, I should like to offer a few, simple, manly explanations."

"Oh, don't apologize."

"Carried away, don't you know. What with the music and the sardine sandwiches."

"That's all right."

"Furthermore, Lottie and I used to be married once, and that forms a sort of bond, if you follow me."

Bill's eyebrows shot up.

"Married?"

"Absolutely married. Long time ago, of course, but somehow the taste still lingered. And when I found her supple form nestling in my arms——"

"Squiffy," said Bill earnestly, "kindly stop apologizing. Nothing could have been more fortunate. It gives me a decent excuse for getting out of an entanglement which has been getting on my nerves for weeks. Lottie's a good sort, but she's too—what's the word?"

"Jumpy?"

"Jumpy is right. When you were married to her, Squiffy, did she ever give you the devil?"

"Frequently."

"For no reason?"

"For no reason whatever."

Bill sighed.

"You know how it is, Squiffy?"

"How what is, old boy?"

"Well, you meet a girl like Lottie and she sweeps you off your feet. And then—well, then you begin to think a bit."

"I see what you mean."

"Besides——"

Bill paused. He, like Squiffy a short while before, seemed embarrassed. He went to the table and drank cold tea.

"Squiffy——"

"Hullo?"

Bill mused for a moment.

"Squiffy——"

"Yes, old man?"

"Squiffy, have you ever felt a sort of strange emptiness in the heart? A sort of aching void of the soul?"

"Oh, rather!"

"What do you do about it?"

"I generally take a couple of cocktails."

Bill shook his head.

"Cocktails aren't any good. Nothing's any good. I've read books, gone in for sport, tried work. No use whatever."

"What sort of work?"

"Stock-farming. And what's the result? I have a thousand pigs, and my heart is empty."

"What you want is a tonic."

"No. I know what I want, Squiffy. I want love."

Lord Tidmouth, that expert, viewed his friend with concern.

"Don't you believe it. Love? Listen, old boy. The amount of love I've had in the last few years, if placed end to end, would reach from London to Paris.

And look at me! Besides, I thought you said you had decided to edge away from Lottie.''

'' Lottie isn't the right girl for me. A good sort— yes. But not the right girl for me. Now, this other girl——''

'' What other girl?''

'' This girl I'm telling you about.''

'' You haven't been telling me about any girl. You haven't so much as mentioned a girl. Do you mean to say——''

Bill nodded.

'' Yes, I've found the real thing at last.''

Lord Tidmouth was interested. He went to the table and with quivering fingers selected a sardine sandwich.

'' Who is she?'' he asked.

'' I don't know. I've only seen her out on the links. She's a poem, Squiffy; all health and fresh air and wholesomeness.''

'' Ever spoken to her?''

'' No, I haven't the nerve. She's so far above me.''

'' Tall girl, eh?''

'' Spiritually, you ass!''

'' Oh, I see.''

There was a pause.

'' I'm going to get to know her somehow,'' said Bill at length.

'' How?''

'' I don't know. But I shall.''

'' And then——''

'' I shall marry her.''

Lord Tidmouth breathed reflectively.

'' Shortly after my arrival in this room,'' he said, '' Lottie gave me to understand that you were practically engaged to marry *her*.''

22

" Yes," said Bill unhappily.

" Then, obviously, what you want to do first," said Lord Tidmouth, " is to get it well into Lottie's mind that it's all off."

" I know. But how?"

" It should be done tactfully."

" Of course."

" Gracefully—kindly—leaving no hard feelings ; but, nevertheless, quite definitely."

" Yes."

Lord Tidmouth pondered.

" Your best plan, old boy," he said, " is to leave the whole thing to me. I understand women. I know exactly the right things to say. Leave the whole thing absolutely and entirely to me, contenting yourself with just murmuring the necessary responses."

Bill brightened.

" You're sure you can manage it?"

" My dear old chap!"

" You'll be tactful?"

" Tactful as dammit. All my wives always raved about my tact. They legged it away from me like rabbits, one after the other, but they always admitted that in the matter of tact I stood alone."

" Well, I'm trusting you."

" And so you may, old boy."

The bedroom door opened and Lottie appeared, dressed for the dance.

CHAPTER III

BILL BANNISTER looked at Lord Tidmouth. He looked appealingly, as a young soldier, in a tight place, might have looked at Napoleon. Lord Tidmouth returned the gaze with a reassuring nod and a leave-it-to-me wave of the hand.

" I'm ready," said Lottie.

Lord Tidmouth eyed her owlishly.

" Ready for what, old thing?"

" To dance."

" With Bill?"

" With Bill."

Tact gleamed from Lord Tidmouth's monocle.

" Bill isn't going to dance."

" But he said he would."

" He's made up his mind to stay in."

" Well, I've made up my face to go out."

" Shall I tell you something, Lottie?" said Lord Tidmouth.

" Go ahead."

" Bill's never going to dance with you again. Never, never again. He's going home. Back to happy Hampshire."

A dangerous gleam appeared in Lottie's beautiful, but formidable, eyes. She directed it at her shrinking playmate.

" Is this true, Bill?"

Bill Bannister er-yessed in a small voice. It was not for him to question the methods of a master of tact like Tidmouth, but he could not restrain a feeling that the news might have been broken a little more gently.

" You see," said Bill, " I simply must go home.

There's the estate to look after and—well, that's all there is to it. I think it's time I went home."

"A thousand pigs are pining for him," said Lord Tidmouth.

"Let me get this straight," said Lottie in a strange, tense voice, not unlike that of a tigress from whom some practical joker is endeavouring to steal the daily ration of meat. "Are you leaving me flat?"

Lord Tidmouth was delighted at his former help-mate's ready intelligence. Of all his wives, he reflected, Lottie had always been quickest at the uptake.

"That's right," he said. "You've put the thing in a nutshell. It's all off, and so is he."

Ignoring a sharp, whistling, sighing noise which proceeded from the lips which had once promised to love, honour, and obey him, he resumed his discourse.

"You see, Bill's a country gentleman, old girl—lives in the wilds, half a dozen miles from anywhere—and he doesn't think you would quite fit into the picture."

"Oh, I'm not fit to associate with his beastly vicars and ploughboys, eh?" asked Lottie, with ominous calm.

"He doesn't say that," urged Lord Tidmouth. "What he means is that you wouldn't be happy in a small village. He's doing you a kindness, really. Why, dash it, if you got fed-up with me in the middle of London, how much fedder-up you would be in a place like Woollam Chersey with a bird like Bill. Good heavens, there's nothing offensive in the man's attitude. He admires and respects you, but he feels that Woollam Chersey is not for you. Lots of the world's most wonderful women would be out of place in Woollam Chersey. Queen Elizabeth—Catherine of Russia—Cleopatra—dozens of them."

He paused, with the complacency of an orator who is conscious of having struck the right note.

"Besides," said Bill, who was not so sure that his collaborator was putting this thing across as well as he thought he was, " if I can't come in without finding you kissing——"

"Old boy!" murmured Lord Tidmouth reproachfully. "Bygones be bygones. Let the dead past bury its dead."

Lottie sniffed.

"So that's the trouble. You know as well as I do that Squiffy means nothing to me any longer. There's no need for you to be jealous."

"I'm not jealous."

"Oh!" said Lottie sharply. "And *why* aren't you, may I ask? I see it all now. There's somebody else."

"No, no," said Lord Tidmouth. "Quite wrong. Absolutely not so."

"There is! Some woman is stealing him away from me." Her voice rose. "Who is she? What's her name? Tell me her name. Who is she?"

She rested her hands on her hips, and from beneath lowering eyebrows glared militantly. Her manner interested Lord Tidmouth, and caused him to advance a theory to explain it.

"I say, Lottie, old girl," asked his lordship, "have you any Spanish blood in you?"

"Now listen, Lottie——"

This from Bill, who was not enjoying the glare.

"I won't listen!"

"My second wife was half Spanish," proceeded Lord Tidmouth chattily. "How well I remember——"

"Shut up!"

"Oh, rather," said his lordship. "I merely spoke."

26

Lottie turned to Bill again.

"So," she said, "you want to get rid of me, do you? You want to throw me aside like a—like a——"

"Worn-out glove," prompted Lord Tidmouth.

"Like a worn-out glove. You think you're going to abandon me like an——"

"Old tube of tooth-paste."

"Shut up!"

"Oh, rather!"

Lottie's eyes flashed.

"Let me tell you you're mistaken if you think you can get rid of *me* so easily."

"Lottie," said Bill, "please!"

"Lottie, please!" said Lord Tidmouth.

"Lottie, please! Lottie, please! Lottie, please!" cried the injured woman in the tones which had intimidated a hundred theatrical dressing-rooms and which when heard during the course of their brief married life by the late Mr. Higginbotham had always been enough to send that pusillanimous cotton magnate shooting off to his club for refuge.

She ran to the tea-table and snatched up a cup.

"There!"

She hurled the cup down with a crash.

"Did you ring, sir?"

It was a bell-boy who spoke. He had appeared in the doorway with a smooth promptness which spoke well for the efficiency of the service at the Superba. This was due partly to long training and partly to the fact that for some moments back he had been standing with his ear glued to the keyhole.

"And there!" cried Lottie, demolishing a second cup.

This one produced Marie.

"Did you call, moddom?"

27

"And there!" said Lottie. "And there! And there!" Another cup, a slop-basin, and the teapot joined the ruins on the floor.

"Lottie," said Bill urgently, "pull yourself together."

"Absolutely," agreed Lord Tidmouth. "Cups cost money—what?"

A piercing scream from the sufferer nearly broke the remaining cup on the table. Marie, advancing solicitously, was just in time to catch her employer as she fell. There was general consternation. All those present were disturbed and distressed, except the bell-boy, who had not had such an enjoyable time since the day, six months ago, when the couple in suite ten had settled a lovers' tiff in his presence with chairs, the leg of a table, and a series of small china ornaments from the mantelpiece.

As always on occasions such as this, the air became full of a babel of words.

"Water!" cried Marie.

"Vinegar!" recommended the bell-boy.

"Eau-de-Cologne!" said Bill.

"Pepper!" said Lord Tidmouth.

Marie had another suggestion.

"Give her air!"

So had the bell-boy.

"Slap her hands!"

Lord Tidmouth went further.

"Sit on her head!" he advised.

The clamour was affecting Bill Bannister's nervous system.

"Will you be quiet?" he roared.

The noise subsided.

"Now then," said Bill, taking command. He turned to the bell-boy. "Go for a doctor."

" Yes, sir."

" And you," continued Bill, addressing Marie, " take her into the bedroom."

" Yes, sir."

The mob scene diminished. Bill, mopping his forehead, was aware of his old friend, Lord Tidmouth, hovering to and fro. He eyed him sourly.

" What are you hanging about for?" he demanded.

Lord Tidmouth reflected.

" Well, honestly, old chap, I don't quite know. Just lending sympathy and moral support, as it were."

" Get a doctor."

" But the boy's getting one."

" Well, get another. Get a dozen."

Lord Tidmouth patted Bill's shoulder with infinite gentleness and understanding.

" I know just how you're feeling, old boy," he said. " You've never seen Lottie in quite this frame of mind before, and you find it upsetting. To me, of course, all this is old stuff. How well I remember," said Lord Tidmouth, beginning to dictate his autobiography, " how clearly it all comes back, that second week of our honeymoon when, in a spirit of kindly criticism, I told her that her new hat looked like nothing on earth. People talk about the San Francisco earthquake——"

" Get *out*!"

" Just as you say, old boy."

" And don't come back without a doctor."

" I won't," Lord Tidmouth assured him. " I'll get one if I have to rob a hospital. For the moment, then, laddie, tinkerty-tonk!"

The room now empty, Bill felt more composed. He called sharply to Marie, who popped out of the bedroom like a cuckoo from a clock.

29

" Marie! "

" Sir? "

" How is she? "

" Still unconscious, sir. And I don't like her breathing. If you ask me, it's storterous."

" Storterous? "

" Sort of puffy. Like this."

Taking in a supply of air, Marie emitted it in a series of moaning gasps. It was not an inartistic performance, but Bill did not like it.

" Marie! "

" Sir? "

" When I want any farmyard imitations I'll ask for them."

" Very good, sir."

Hurt by destructive criticism, the maid withdrew into the bedroom. The door had scarcely closed behind her when the bell-boy appeared. He had the unmistakable look of a bell-boy who is about to deliver the goods.

" The doctor, sir," he announced, with modest pride.

Bill heaved a relieved sigh.

" Send him in," he said.

And, having said it, he stood gaping. Framed in the doorway was a young and becomingly dressed girl. She carried a small black bag, and at the sight of her Bill Bannister's eyes widened to an incredulous stare and his jaw drooped like a lily. Then there swept over him so tumultuous a rush of ecstasy that his vocal cords seemed tangled in a knot.

He swallowed convulsively, and realized despairingly that speech for the moment was entirely beyond him.

30

CHAPTER IV

SALLY eyed him composedly. She had been going out for a walk when the bell-boy found her, and she was anxious to finish the task before her and resume that walk as quickly as possible. Of the emotions surging in Bill's soul she had no inkling. She certainly had never seen him before in her life, and was not excited by the sight of him now. She had set him down at a glance as one of those typical, pleasant, idle, young men whose charm made so slight an impression on her. Only workers interested Sally Smith.

She was on the point of coming briskly to business when the extraordinary pop-eyed nature of his stare forced itself on her attention. A moment later he advanced a step towards her, still looking like a prawn, and in an odd, strangled voice emitted the single word "Guk!"

That, at least, was how it sounded to Sally. She raised her eyebrows.

"I beg your pardon?" she said.

Bill Bannister, with a supreme effort, had now got his Adam's apple back into position and regained control of his vocal cords. But even now the sight of this girl rendered speaking difficult. At close range, he found himself observing things about her which had escaped him at a distance. Her nose, which he had supposed straight, turned up at the tip. He had never seen her teeth before. He liked them.

"It can't be!" he said.

"I don't quite understand," said Sally.

Nor did she. This man seemed *non compos.*

31

"I—er—mean," said Bill. "What I mean is
. . . I've seen you before."

"Really? Where?"

"Out on the links."

"Yes, I've been playing quite a lot."

"Yes," said Bill. "I saw you there. . . . Out
on the links. . . . I saw you several times out on
the links."

He paused a moment, wishing to make his meaning
clearer.

"You were out on the links," he said. "And I
saw you."

"I see," said Sally. "And now where is my
patient?"

"Patient?"

"I was told that someone here wanted a doctor."

"Yes. A—sort of friend of mine has had a kind
of nervous breakdown."

"A female friend, I suppose?"

"Er—yes."

"Well, hadn't I better see her?"

A bright light shone upon Bill.

"You don't mean to say you're a doctor?"

"I do."

"Gosh! I mean—I say, do sit down, won't
you?"

"I really can't waste time like this," said Sally
coldly. That "gosh!" had had its usual effect on
her equanimity. "If you don't want me to attend
the patient I'll go."

"But—she can't see a doctor now."

"Why not?"

"She isn't well."

Sally's momentary pique faded. This extraordinary
young man amused her.

" My dear good man," she said, " are you always like this, or have I just struck one of your bad days?"

Bill writhed.

" I know I'm an idiot——"

" Ah, a lucid moment."

" It's the shock of seeing you walk in like this."

" Why shouldn't I walk in? You sent for me."

" Yes, but you don't understand. I mean, I've seen you out on the golf-links."

" So you said before."

" You see, Mrs.——"

" Miss."

" Thank God!"

" I beg your pardon?"

" Nothing, nothing. I—er—that is to say—er—putting it rather differently—— Oh, my goodness!"

" What's the matter?"

" You take my breath away."

" For shortness of breath try a jujube. And now, please, my patient."

" Oh, yes. . . ."

Bill went to the door of the bedroom and called softly.

" Marie!"

Marie appeared in the doorway.

" Yes, sir?"

" How is she?"

" Asleep, sir."

" Fine!" said Bill, brightening. " See that she doesn't wake up." He came back to Sally. " The maid says the patient has fallen asleep."

Sally nodded.

" Quite natural. Sleep often follows violent hysteria."

" But, I say, how do you know it was hysteria?"

" By the broken china. Long-distance diagnosis. Well, let her have her sleep out."

" I will."

There was a pause.

" Tea," said Bill, at length, desperately. " Won't you have some tea?"

" Where is it?"

Bill looked about him.

" Well, on the floor, mostly," he admitted. " But I could ring for some more."

" Don't bother. I don't like tea much, anyway."

" You're American, aren't you?"

" I am."

" It's a rummy thing, Americans never seem very keen on tea."

" No?"

There was another pause.

" I say," said Bill, " I didn't get your name."

" Doctor Sally Smith. What's yours?"

" Bannister—William Bannister."

" You live here?"

" Certainly not," said Bill, shocked. " I'm staying at the ' Majestic '. I live down in Hampshire."

" One of these big country houses, I suppose?"

" Pretty big."

" I thought so. You look opulent," said Sally, pleased that her original opinion had been confirmed.

A rich idler, this man, she felt. Not unpleasant, it was true—she liked his face and was amused by him —but nevertheless idle and rich.

Bill, by this time, had gradually become something more nearly resembling a sentient being. Indeed, he was now quite at his ease again and feeling extraordinarily happy. That this girl and he should be sitting chatting together like this was so wonderful that it put him right on top of his form. He straightened his tie and threw his whole soul into one devoted gaze.

Sally got the gaze, and did not like it. For some moments now she had been wishing that this perfect stranger would either make his eyes rather less soulful or else refrain from directing them at her. She was a liberal-minded girl and did not disapprove of admiration from the other sex; indeed, she had grown accustomed to exciting it; but something seemed to whisper to her that this William Bannister could do with a little womanly quelling.

"Would you mind not looking at me like that?" she said coolly.

The soulful look faded out of Bill's eyes, as if he had been hit between them by a brick. He felt disconcerted and annoyed. He disliked being snubbed, even by a girl for whom his whole being yearned.

"I'm not looking at you like that," he replied with spirit. "At least, I'm not trying to."

Sally nodded tolerantly.

"I see," she said. "Automatic, eh? Very interesting, from a medical point of view. Unconscious reaction of the facial and labial muscles at sight of a pretty woman."

Bill's pique increased. He resented this calm treating of himself as something odd on a microscopic slide.

"I am sorry," he said haughtily, "if I embarrassed you."

Sally laughed.

"You didn't embarrass me," she said. "Did I seem to you to show embarrassment? I thought I had my vascular motors under much better control."

"Your what did you say?"

"Vascular motors. They regulate the paling and flushing of the skin. In other words, I didn't blush."

35

"Oh, ah! I see."

The conversation flagged again.

"Do you know," said Bill, hoisting it to its legs again, "I was most awfully surprised when you said you were a doctor?"

"Most men seem to be."

"I mean, you don't look like a doctor."

"How ought a doctor to look?"

Bill reflected.

"Well, most of them seem sort of fagged and over-worked. Haggard chaps. I mean, it must be an awful strain."

Sally laughed.

"Oh, it's not so bad. You needn't waste your pity on me, Mr. Bannister. I'm as fit as a fiddle, thank heaven, and enjoy every minute of my life. I have a good practice and quite enough money. I go to theatres and concerts. I play games. I spend my vacations travelling. I love my work. I love my recreations. I love life."

"You're wonderful!"

"And why shouldn't I? I earn every bit of pleasure that I get. I like nice clothes, nice shoes, nice stockings—because I buy them myself. I'm like the village blacksmith—I owe not any man. I wonder if you've the remotest idea how happy it can make a woman feel just to be a worker and *alive*—with good nerves, good circulation, and good muscles. Feel my arm. Like iron."

"Wonderful!"

"And my legs. Hard as a rock. Prod 'em."

"No, really!"

"Go on."

She looked at him with amusement.

"You're blushing!"

36

Bill was unable to deny the charge.

"Yes," he said. "I'm afraid my vascular motors aren't as well controlled as yours."

"Can't you admire a well-rounded, highly perfected leg in a purely detached spirit as a noble work of nature?"

"Sorry—no. I'm afraid I've never quite managed to do that."

"Why, in some countries the women go swimming with nothing on."

"And the men buy telescopes."

"Don't snigger."

"Forgive me," said Bill. "I laugh, like Figaro, that I may not weep."

She regarded him curiously.

"What do you want to weep about?"

Bill sighed.

"I'm feeling a little depressed," he said. "In the life you have outlined—this hard, tense, independent, self-sufficing life, with its good nerves and good circulation and muscles of the brawny arm as strong as iron bands, don't you think—it's just a suggestion—don't you think there's something a little *bleak*?"

"Bleak?"

"Well, frankly——"

"Always be frank."

"Frankly, then," said Bill, "it reminds me of the sort of nightmare H. G. Wells would have after cold pork. It seems to leave out the one thing that makes life worth living."

"You mean love?"

"Exactly. I grant you one hundred per cent on nerves and circulation and general fitness. I admire your biceps, I'm sure your leg-muscle is all it should be, and I take off my hat to your vascular motors—

but doesn't it strike you that you're just the merest trifle lacking in *sentiment*?"

She frowned.

"Nothing of the kind. All I'm lacking in is sentimentality. I don't droop and blush and giggle——"

"No, I noticed that."

"—But naturally I don't intend to exclude love from my life. I'm not such a fool."

"Ah!"

"Why do you say 'Ah'?"

A touch of dignity came into Bill's manner.

"Listen," he said. "You're the loveliest girl I ever met, but you've got to stop bullying me. I shall say 'Ah!' just as often as I please."

"I merely asked because most people when they stand in front of me and say 'Ah', expect me to examine their throats."

She paused.

"Why are you so interested in my views on love, Mr. Bannister?" she asked casually.

Even Bill, quick worker though he had been from boyhood, would have shrunk—had the conditions been other than they were—from laying bare his soul at this extremely early point in his association with this girl. Emotion might have urged him to do so, but Prudence would have plucked at his sleeve. So intense, however, was his desire to shatter his companion's maddening aloofness—at least, was aloofness exactly the word?—dispassionate friendliness described it better —no, *detached*—that was the word he wanted; she was so cool and detached and seemed so utterly oblivious to the importance of a Bannister's yearnings that he let Emotion have its way. And if Prudence did any plucking, he failed to notice it.

"I'll tell you why," he said explosively. "Because the moment I saw you out there on the links I knew you were the one girl——"

" You mean you've fallen in love with me?"

" I have. The news doesn't seem to surprise you," said Bill resentfully.

Sally laughed.

" Oh, it's not such a terrible shock."

" You've heard the same sort of thing before from other men, I suppose?"

" Dozens of times."

" I might have known it," said Bill gloomily. " Just my luck. And I suppose——"

" No. You're wrong."

Bill became animated again.

" You mean there's nobody else?"

" Nobody."

Bill's animation approached fever point.

" Then do you think—do you suppose—might it happen—would it be—er—putting it another way, is it possible——"

" Crisper, crisper, and simpler. What you're trying to suggest now is that perhaps I might one day love you? Am I right?"

" You take the words out of my mouth."

" I had to, or they would never have emerged at all. Well, if I ever love a man I shall inform him of the fact, simply and naturally, as if I were saying good morning."

Bill hesitated.

" Tell me," he said, " have you ever—er—wished a man good morning?"

" No. That experience has yet to come."

" Wonderful!"

" Not so very wonderful. It simply means I haven't met the right man."

39

Bill could not allow a totally false statement like this to pass uncorrected.

"Yes, you have," he assured her. "You don't know it yet, but you have." He advanced towards her, full of his theme.

"You have really. Oh," said Bill. He drew a deep breath. "Gosh!" he exclaimed, "I feel as if a great weight had rolled off me. I had always hoped in my heart that women like you existed, and now it's all come true. Don't laugh at me. It's come upon me like a whirlwind. I never expected it. I never guessed. I never——"

"Excuse me, sir," said Marie, appearing at the bed-room door.

CHAPTER V

BILL regarded her with marked displeasure. In the past Marie had always seemed to him rather a nice girl, but now he felt he had seldom encountered a more pronounced pest.

"Well," he said irritably, "what is it?"

"If you please, sir, she's awake now."

Bill could make nothing of this. The girl appeared to him to be babbling. Sheer gossip from the padded cell.

"Awake?" he said. "What on earth are you talking about? Who's awake?"

"Why, moddom, sir."

Bill blinked like an awkward somnambulist.

"Moddom?"

Sally laughed.

"I think you had forgotten our patient, hadn't you?"

She turned briskly to Marie.

"Ask her to come in, please. I will examine her at once."

It was a calmer and more subdued Lottie who emerged from the bedroom. But it was plain that the volcano was not altogether extinct. In her manner, as she suddenly beheld a charming and attractive girl in Bill's society in her sitting-room there were obvious indications that something of the old fire still lingered. She stiffened. She glared in hostile fashion. Bill, watching, was disturbed to see her hands go to her hips in a well-remembered gesture.

"Oh!" said Lottie. "And who may this be?"

"I'm the doctor," said Sally.

41

"You think I'm going to swallow that?"

Sally sighed resignedly.

"Can you read?"

"Of course I can read."

"Then read that," said Sally, producing a card.

Lottie scrutinized it doubtfully. Then her manner changed.

"Doctor Sally Smith," she said. "Well, I suppose that's all right. Still, it looks funny to me. And let me tell you that if there is any funny business going on between you two, I'll very soon——"

"Quiet, please," said Sally.

She spoke calmly, but the speaker stopped as if she had run into a brick wall.

"I want to make an examination," said Sally.

"Perhaps I'd better leave you?" said Bill.

"Just as you like."

"I'll go for a stroll on the front."

"All right," said Sally. "I shan't be long."

She put her stethoscope together as the door closed. Lottie, having recovered, felt disposed for conversation.

"You'll forgive me, I'm sure, doctor——" She paused. "Isn't that too silly of me—I've forgotten your damn name."

"It's quite an easy one to remember," said Sally, busy with her stethoscope. "Smith."

Lottie beamed.

"Oh, thank you! I was saying, doctor, that I was sure you'd forgive me for flying off the handle a little just now. The fact is I've just been having a bit of a row with Mr. Bannister, and coming in and finding you two together like that naturally I said to my-self——"

"Take off that bath-robe."

"Eh? Oh, all right. Let me see, where was I? What started it all was him saying to me—or rather Squiffy did, and he didn't contradict it—that he wasn't ever going to take me dancing again. 'Oh,' I said, 'and why not, may I ask?' 'I'm going home,' he said. 'Going home?' I said. 'Yes,' he said, 'going home.' So naturally I said, 'I know what the trouble with *you* is,' I said; 'you want to cast me off like a worn-out glove. But if you think for one moment that I'm going to stand anything like that——' "

"The lungs appear sound," said Sally.

" 'You're mistaken,' I said——"

"Take a deep breath. Well, the heart seems all right. Now for the reflexes. Cross your legs. . . . Nothing the matter with them. All right, that's all."

"Examination over?"

"Yes."

Lottie became interested.

"What's wrong with me?"

"Nothing much. You need a rest."

"Aren't you going to look at my tongue?"

"I can tell, without looking at it, that that needs a rest too. What you want is a few weeks in a nice, quiet sanatorium."

"You're going to send me to a sanatorium?"

"Well, I'm advising you to go. You need a place where there are cold baths and plain food, and no cocktails and cigarettes."

Lottie shuddered.

"It sounds like hell!" she said. She frowned. "I believe it's a trick."

"A trick?"

"I believe you're just trying to get me out of the way so that you can have him to yourself."

"Him?" Sally stared. "You can't mean——

43

Do you really imagine for one moment that I'm in love with Mr. Bannister?"

" You aren't?"

" Of course not."

" And you want me to go to a sanatorium?"

" I think you ought to."

" Well," said Lottie, " it all looks funny to *me*!"

The door opened and Lord Tidmouth appeared. He seemed pleased with himself.

" Hullo!" said Lord Tidmouth. " I say, I've snaffled a medicine-man." His eye rested on Sally. He stared. " Hullo!"

Sally returned his gaze composedly.

" I have already examined the patient," she said.

" *You* have?" said Lord Tidmouth, perplexed.

" Yes. My name is Doctor Smith."

" *Doctor* Smith?"

" Doctor Smith."

Lord Tidmouth's was not a very agile brain, but it was capable of flashes of intuition.

" You mean *you're* a doctor?" he said brightly.

" Yes."

" I see. Of course," said Lord Tidmouth, with the air of a man who is always prepared to listen to reason, " there *are* lady doctors."

" Yes. I'm one of them."

" Absolutely. Yes, I see your point. I say," said Lord Tidmouth, " this is rather awkward. Old Bill sent me to get a doctor, and I grabbed one in the lobby."

" I'm afraid there's nothing for him to do here."

" Not a thing," agreed Lottie. " What do you think I'm doing here, Squiffy, you poor nut—holding a medical convention?"

44

Lord Tidmouth rubbed his chin.

"But he's apt to be a bit shirty, isn't he, if he finds I've lugged him up here for nothing? He wasn't any too pleased at having to come at all. He was on his way to the links."

"Oh, well," said Sally, sympathizing with his concern, "as you've called him in, we can have a consultation, if he likes. Where is he?"

"Navigating the stairs. Stout old boy, not very quick on his pins." He went to the door. "This way, doc," he called.

A puffing noise without announced that the medicine-man was nearing journey's end. The next moment he had entered, and Sally, turning to the door, was surprised to find that this was no stranger in her midst but an old acquaintance.

"Why, Sir Hugo!" she said.

Sir Hugo Drake had just enough breath left to say, "God bless my soul! You here?" After that he resumed his puffing.

Lord Tidmouth became apologetic.

"I'm awfully sorry," he said, addressing his panting captive. "I'm afraid there's been a mis-understanding."

"This gentleman," explained Sally, "didn't know that I was here."

"No," said his lordship. "The whole trouble was, you see, Old Bill got the wind up and sent the entire strength of the company out scouring the town for medicos. It begins to look like a full house."

Sir Hugo realized the position.

"No need for me at all, eh? Well, I'm just as pleased. I've an appointment on the links. Of course, if you'd like a consultation——"

"Could you spare the time?" asked Sally.

" Certainly, if you wish it.   Mustn't take too long, though."

" Oh, of course not; only a few minutes."

" Very well, then.   This young lady the patient?"

" Yes."

" Well, step into the bedroom, young lady, and we'll go into your case."

Lottie rose obediently.   She was feeling a little flattered at this inrush of doctors on her behalf.

" She says I ought to go into a sanatorium," she said, indicating Sally.

" Subject to Sir Hugo's opinion," said Sally.

Sir Hugo nodded.

" Oh, we'll thrash the whole thing out, never fear. We'll go into the case minutely.   Run along, my dear."

" Well, I ought to be all right between the two of you," said Lottie, and closed the bedroom door behind her.

Lord Tidmouth seemed relieved that matters had reached such an amicable settlement.   He had had visions of this red-faced bird setting about him with a niblick.

" Then I'll leave you to it—what?   I've often wondered," he said meditatively, " what you doctors talk about when you hold consultations.   Lot of deep stuff, I expect."

CHAPTER VI

FOR a moment after the departure of Lord Tidmouth there was silence in the room. Sir Hugo was still engaged in recovering his full supply of breath. This done, he looked at Sally inquiringly.

"What's the trouble?"

"Oh, nothing," said Sally. "Just a little nervous."

Sir Hugo cocked an eye at the debris on the floor.

"Seems to have been violent."

"Yes. That type. Too many cocktails and cigarettes, and no self-restraint. I thought she ought to have a few weeks' rest."

"I imagined from the way that young fellow snatched me up and carried me off that it was a matter of life and death. Silly idiot! Now I shall be late for my golf match."

"How did you get on this morning after you left me?" asked Sally.

Sir Hugo sighed, as Napoleon might have sighed if somebody had met him after the battle of Waterloo and asked, "Well, how did it all come out?"

"He beat me four and three."

"What a shame!"

"I didn't seem able to do anything right," said Sir Hugo, wallowing in this womanly sympathy. "If I didn't hook I sliced. And if I didn't slice I topped."

"That's too bad."

"I only needed a nine to win the fourteenth, and I ought to have got it easily. But I blew up on the green."

" That's often the way, isn't it?"

" Mark you," said Sir Hugo, " I wasn't so bad off
the tee. Some of my drives were extremely good. It
was the short shots that beat me—just the ones you
are so wonderful at. If I could play my mashie as
you do, my handicap would be down below twenty
before I knew where I was."

" What do you find is the trouble? Shanking?"

" No, topping, principally."

" You oughtn't to look up."

" I know I oughtn't, but I do."

" Do you think you are gripping right?" asked
Sally.

" Well, I'm *gripping*," said Sir Hugo. " I don't
know if I'm doing it right."

" Would you like me to show you?"

" My dear young lady, I should like it above all
things!"

A monocled head appeared round the edge of the
door. Curiosity had been too much for Lord Tidmouth.

" How are you getting on?" he inquired.

" Kindly leave us alone, young man," said Sir
Hugo, testily. " We are at a very difficult point in
the diagnosis."

" Oh, right-ho. Poo-boop-a-doop," said Lord
Tidmouth amiably, and vanished again.

Sir Hugo turned to Sally.

" You were saying you would show me——"

Sally stretched out a hand towards the golf-bag.

" May I borrow one of your clubs?" she said.
" Now, then. So much depends on the right grip.
Do you use the Vardon?"

" I used to, but lately I've gone back to the
double-V."

48

"Well, the great thing is not to grip too tightly. Grip firmly but lightly."

"Firmly but lightly. I see."

"The hands should be kept low, and, above all, should finish low. So many people finish their iron shots with the hands up, as if they were driving."

"True," said Sir Hugo. "True."

"At the finish of the chip-shot the club should be very little above the horizontal. Not like in the drive."

Sir Hugo nodded.

"I see. Talking of driving, it may interest you to hear of a little experience I had the other day. I had made my drive——"

"A rather similar thing once happened to me," said Sally. "It was this way——"

"I went to play my second," proceeded Sir Hugo, who may not have been much good as a golfer, but stood almost alone as a golf bore. A man who had out-talked tough, forceful men in clubs, he was not going to let himself be silenced by a mere girl. "I went to play my second, and, believe me or believe me not——"

"What do you think?" said Sally. "I found——"

"I just——"

"I simply——"

The bedroom door opened abruptly.

"Haven't you two finished yet?" asked Lottie peevishly.

Sir Hugo started like one awakened from a beautiful dream.

"Oh, quite, quite," he said, embarrassed. "We were just about to call you. We've examined your case from every angle——"

"And Sir Hugo agrees with me——" said Sally.

49

" Exactly. That your trouble——"

" Is a slight matter of nerves——"

" Nothing of any consequence, though disagreeable——"

" And you must be kept in a sanatorium——"

" Firmly but lightly," said Sir Hugo. " I mean —ah—just so."

Lord Tidmouth manifested himself again.

" Hullo!" he said. " Consultation over?"

" Yes," said Lottie. " They say I ought to go to a sanatorium."

" I can recommend this one," said Sir Hugo. " I will write down the address."

" Oh, all right," said Lottie. " Leave it on the table. I'm going out."

" To find Bill?" said Lord Tidmouth. " He's probably on the front somewhere."

Lottie laughed a bitter laugh.

" Bill? I don't want Bill. I've nothing to say to Mr. Bannister. If I'm to be dumped in a sanatorium, I'm going to get in a bit of dancing first. Come along and shake them up, Squiffy?"

" Absolutely," agreed Lord Tidmouth. " Just what the old system needs. Well, toodle-oo everybody."

Sir Hugo was staring open-mouthed at the closed door. He had the air of a man who has received an unpleasant shock.

" *Bannister*, did she say?"

" Yes. Mr. Bannister was here when I came. He went out."

Sir Hugo snorted powerfully.

" So this is the woman he's been fooling around with! I might have guessed it would be some peroxide blonde."

Sally saw daylight.

"Is Mr. Bannister the nephew you were telling me about?"

"He is. And that is the woman! Of all the maddening, worthless nephews a man was ever cursed with——" He paused, and seemed to ponder. "Just show me that grip once more, will you?" he said, coming out of his reverie.

"All right," said Sally agreeably. "But don't you want to worry about your nephew?"

"He can wait," said Sir Hugo grimly.

"I see. Well, give me your hands."

She took his hands and clasped them round the club. And it was in this attitude that Bill, returning for the latest bulletin, found them.

Bill's first emotion was one of excusable wrath at the spectacle. Here was the only girl he had ever really loved, and he had no sooner left her than she started holding hands with a man of advanced years in a suit of plus-fours of the kind that makes horses shy. He cleared his throat austerely, and was about to speak when the plus-foured one turned.

"William!" he said, and Bill wilted.

If one of the more austere of the minor prophets had worn plus-fours he would have looked just as Sir Hugo Drake was looking now. The great specialist had drawn himself up, and he could not have regarded Bill more sternly if the latter had been a germ.

"So I've found you, have I!"

"Oh, hullo, uncle!" said Bill.

"Don't say 'Oh, hullo, uncle!' to me," boomed Sir Hugo. "This is a pleasant surprise for a man who stands *in loco parentis*, is it not? I come down here to this place, to this Bingley-on-Sea, and before

I've hardly had time to put a ball down on the first tee I am called in to attend to your female associates!"

"Uncle, please!"

Sir Hugo strode to the door.

"I am returning to Woollam Chersey to-night, William," he said. "I shall expect you to accompany me."

"I can't!"

"Why not?"

Bill looked helplessly at Sally.

"I'll be back in a day or two," he said.

"Then I shall remain till you leave," said Sir Hugo. "And let me tell you, I shall watch this suite like a hawk."

"There's no *need* for you to watch this suite——"

"There is every need for me to watch this suite. Good God, boy, I've seen the female! If you imagine that I'm going to stand idly by and see you get yourself inextricably entangled with a woman who dyes her hair and throws tea-cups about hotels you are vastly mistaken." He looked at his watch. "Great heavens! Is that the time? I must fly. I'll remember what you told me about that grip. Firmly but lightly. Hands not too much over. William, I shall be seeing you again. We will discuss this affair then."

Although his uncle—corporeally considered—had left him, his aura of influence seemed still to oppress William Bannister. He gulped once or twice before speaking.

"How on earth did he get here?" he gasped.

"Lord Tidmouth found him in the lobby and dragged him up," said Sally. "Poor Mr. Bannister, you don't have much luck with your medical advisers, do you?'' She moved towards the door. ''Well, good-bye.''

Bill quivered.

'' You're not going?''

'' Yes, I am. Will you give me your address.''

'' Woollam Chersey, Hampshire, finds me.'' He drew a deep breath. '' How wonderful! You want to write to me?''

'' No. I just want to know where to send my bill.''

'' Good heavens!''

'' What's the matter?''

Bill walked across to the sofa and kicked it violently.

'' It's enough to drive a man mad,'' he said. '' Whenever I say anything—anything with any sentiment in it—you immediately become the doctor, and freeze me with a cold douche.''

'' What do you expect me to do—swoon in your arms?''

'' You haven't an atom of feeling in you.''

'' Oh, yes, I have. And some day the right man will bring it out. Cheer up, Mr. Bannister. You look like a sulky baby that's been refused its bottle.'' She laughed. '' I think your uncle's quite right, and you're still a small boy.''

Bill scowled.

'' Oh, I'll prove to you some day that I'm grown up.''

Sally laughed again.

'' Oh, I'm not saying you may not grow up some day. But at present you're just a child.''

'' I'm not.''

'' You are.''

'' I'm not.''

'' Yes, you are.''

53

There was a knock at the door. The bell-boy entered.

"Please, sir," said the bell-boy, "your rocking-horse has arrived."

"What!" cried Bill.

"There!" said Sally.

Bill passed a hand through his disordered hair.

"My rocking-horse? What do you mean, my rocking-horse?"

"Well, all I know is there's a rocking-horse outside. Shall I bring it in?"

"No!" cried Bill.

"Yes," said Sally. "Good-bye, Mr. Bannister. Naturally you will want to be alone. You don't want grown-ups around at a moment like this. Good-bye."

"Come back!" shouted Bill.

But Sally had gone.

CHAPTER VII

IF there was a thought in the mind of Lord Tidmouth as he sat, some two weeks after his visit to Bingley-on-Sea, playing solitaire in the living-hall of his friend Bill Bannister's country-seat at Woollam Chersey in the county of Hampshire, it was a vaguely formulated feeling that life was extremely pleasant, and that there was no getting away from it that these all-male parties were the best. He had had an excellent dinner, the lamps were lit, and it seemed to him that there was nothing whatever to worry about in the world.

Lord Tidmouth liked peace and quiet. Women, in his experience, militated against an atmosphere of quiet peace. Look at his second wife, for instance. For the matter of that, look at his third and fourth. He was placidly content that the Manor, Woollam Chersey, harboured, beside himself, only William, his host, inert now in a neighbouring arm-chair, and William's uncle, Sir Hugo Drake, at present occupied in the passage without, practising putts into a tumbler.

The room in which Bill and Lord Tidmouth sat was old and panelled. Its furniture was masculine and solid. From the walls portraits of dead-and-gone Bannisters gazed down, and in one corner there was a suit of armour which it was Lord Tidmouth's practice to tap smartly whenever he passed it. He liked the ringing sound it gave out. What with an occasional tap on this suit of armour, plenty to eat and drink, and sufficient opportunities for playing solitaire, Lord Tidmouth found life at Woollam Chersey satisfactory.

A kindly soul, he wished he could have thought that his host was in a similar frame of mind. As far as he

55

allowed himself to worry about anything, he was a little worried about good old Bill. The man seemed on edge. Very far from his merry self he had been since that afternoon at Bingley. This troubled Lord Tidmouth at times.

It did not, however, trouble him to the extent of spoiling his enjoyment in his game of solitaire. With pursed lips he uncovered a card, held it in the air, put it on one of the piles, removed a second card from another pile and put it on a third pile—in fact, went through all the movements peculiar to those addicted to this strange game.

It is almost inevitable that a man who is playing solitaire will sooner or later sing. Lord Tidmouth, who had for some little time been humming in an undertone, now came boldly into the open and committed himself to the rendition of a popular ballad:

" I fee-ar naw faw in shee-ining arr-mour,
Though his lance be swift and—er—keen . . ."

In his arm-chair Bill stirred uneasily.

" But I fee-ar, I fee-ar the glarr-moor
Ther-oo thy der-ooping larr-shes seen,
I fee-ar, I fee-ar, the glar-moor . . ."

" Oh, shut up!" said Bill.

Lord Tidmouth, ceasing to sing, turned amiably.

" Sorry, old top," he said. " I thought you were dead."

" What are you doing?"

" Playing solitaire, laddie." He fiddled with the cards, and absently burst into song once more:

" Just playing sol-i-taire. . . ."

" Stop it!"

" Stop playing?"

56

"Stop yowling."

"Oh, right-ho."

Bill rose and surveyed the card-strewn table with an unfriendly eye.

"Do you mean to say you really get any pleasure out of that rotten game?"

"Darned good game," protested Lord Tidmouth. He manipulated the cards. "Did you ever hear the story of the ventriloquist who played solitaire? He used to annoy his wife by holding long conversations with himself in his sleep. It became such a trial to the poor woman that she had serious thoughts of getting a divorce. And then one evening, by the greatest good luck, he caught himself cheating at solitaire, and never spoke to himself again."

"Silly idiot!"

"Harsh words, old man, from host to guest. Nice place you've got here, Bill."

"Glad you like it."

"Been in the family quite a time, I take it?"

"A few centuries."

Bill's manner became furtive. He glanced to and fro in a conspiratorial fashion. It seemed that whatever had been on his mind all the evening was coming to a head.

"Squiffy!"

"Hullo?"

"Where's my uncle?"

"Out in the corridor putting vigorously. What a man!"

"Thank God, that'll keep him occupied for a while. Squiffy, there's something I want to tell you."

"Carry on, old boy."

"To-night I——"

He broke off. A stout figure, swathed in a

57

mauve smoking-jacket and carrying a putter, had entered.

" It's coming!" said Sir Hugo Drake joyfully. " The knack is coming. I'm getting it. Four out of my last seven shots straight into the glass."

" I think I'll take a shot in a glass myself," said Lord Tidmouth, rising and making for the table where the decanter and siphon so invitingly stood.

" I fancy I have at last found out what has been wrong with my putting. . . . William!"

" Hullo?"

" I say I think I have at last found out what has been wrong with my putting."

" Oh!"

" I've been gripping too tight. How right that girl was. ' Grip firmly but lightly,' she said; ' that's the secret.' It stands to reason——"

" Excuse me," said Bill, and removed himself with the smooth swiftness of a family ghost.

Sir Hugo stood staring after him. This was not the first time activity of this sort had suddenly descended upon his nephew in the middle of a conversation. He did not like it. Apart from the incivility of it, it seemed to him ominous. He confided this fear to Lord Tidmouth, who was still occupied with his spot.

" Lord Tidmouth!"

His companion lowered his glass courteously.

" Present!" he said. " Here in person."

Sir Hugo jerked a thumb towards the door.

" Did you see that?"

" What?"

" Did you see the curious, sudden way that boy left the room?"

" He did move fairly nippily," agreed Lord Tidmouth. "Now you saw him and now you didn't, as it were."

"He has been like that ever since he got home—nervous, rude, jumpy, abrupt."

"Yes, I've noticed he's been a bit jumpy."

"What do you suppose is the matter with him?"

"Not been eating enough yeast," said Lord Tidmouth confidently.

"No! He's in love."

"You think so?"

"I'm sure of it. I noticed it the day I arrived here. I had begun to tell him about the long brassie-shot I made at the sixteenth hole and he gave a sort of hollow gasp and walked away."

"Walked away?"

"Walked away in the middle of a sentence. The boy's in love. There can be no other explanation."

Lord Tidmouth considered.

"Now I come to remember it, he did say something to me down at that seaside place about being in love."

"I was sure of it. William is pining for that peroxide woman."

"You mean Lottie?"

"The flashy young person I sent to the sanatorium."

"I don't think so. I have an idea he told me he was in love with someone else."

Sir Hugo was not a man who took kindly to having his diagnoses questioned.

"Absurd! Nothing of the kind. Do you think I don't know what I'm talking about? He was infatuated with that young woman then, and he's still infatuated with her. Possibly we ought not to be surprised. After all, they parted only a mere two weeks ago. But I confess I am much disturbed."

"What are you going to do about it?"

A senile cunning gleamed from Sir Hugo's eyes.

"Rather ask what I have done about it."

"Well, what have you done about it?"

"Never mind."

"Then why did you tell me to ask?" said Lord Tidmouth, justly aggrieved.

He went to the table and mixed himself another whisky-and-soda with an injured air. Sir Hugo was far too occupied to observe it.

"Young man," he said, "have you ever studied psychology?"

"Psy——"

"——chology."

Lord Tidmouth shook his head.

"Well, no," he said, "not to any great extent. They didn't teach me much at school except the difference between right and wrong. There *is* some difference, but I've forgotten what."

"Have you ever asked yourself what is the secret of the glamour which this young woman exercises over William?"

"I suppose it's the same she used to exercise over *me*. Used to be married to her once, don't you know?"

"What!"

"Oh, yes. But it blew over."

Sir Hugo considered this unforeseen piece of information. He seemed to be turning it over in his mind.

"I cannot decide whether that is good or bad."

"Bit of both, I found it."

"I mean, whether it helps my plan or not."

"What plan?"

"It is based on psychology. I ask myself, 'What is this young person's attraction for William based on?'"

60

" Psychology?" asked Lord Tidmouth, who was becoming fogged.

" It is due to the fact that he has encountered her so far only in the gaudy atmosphere of hotels and dance-halls—her natural setting. But suppose he should see her in the home of his ancestors, where every stick and stone breathes of family traditions, beneath the eyes of the family portraits? What then?"

" I'll bite. What?"

" She would disgust him. His self-respect would awaken. The scales would fall from his eyes, and his infatuation would wither and decay. Whatever his faults, William is a Bannister."

" In that case it might be a sound scheme to invite her down here for a visit."

Sir Hugo chuckled.

" Ha, ha! Young man, can you keep a secret?"

" I don't know. I've never tried."

" Well, let me tell you this, Lord Tidmouth. I have the situation well in hand. Youth," said Sir Hugo, " may fancy it can control its own destiny, but age, with its riper wisdom, is generally able, should the occasion arise, to lay it a stymie. Excuse me, I must go and putt."

CHAPTER VIII

LORD TIDMOUTH resumed his solitaire. He was glad Sir Hugo had left him. He had nothing specific against the old buster, but it was pleasanter to be alone. Presently he was deep in his game once more, and singing like a nightingale.

" *My strength's a something—something . . .*"

sang Lord Tidmouth. And then, more confidently, as one feeling himself on secure ground:

" *And a right good shield of hides untanned. . . .*"

He put a red five on a black six.

" *And a right good shield of hides untanned. . . .*"

A four of clubs went on the red five.

"*Which on my arm I ber-huckle. . . .*"

A slight but definite sound as of one in pain, coming from his immediate rear, aroused him, and he turned. He perceived his friend William Bannister.

" Hullo, Bill, old man! You back?"

Bill was looking cautiously about him.

" Where's my uncle?"

" Just oozed off. Want me to call him?"

" Good heavens, no! Squiffy——"

" Hullo?"

Bill did not reply for a few moments. These moments he occupied in wandering in a rather feverish manner about the room, fiddling with various objects that came in his path. He halted at the mantelpiece, gazed for a while at the portrait of his great-grandfather which hung above it; quickly wearied of the spectacle and resumed his prowling. Lord Tidmouth watched him with growing disapproval. Between Sir Hugo Drake and this William his quiet, peaceful evening was being entirely disorganized.

"Squiffy!" said Bill, halting suddenly.

"Still here," replied Lord Tidmouth plaintively. "What's the idea? Training for a marathon?"

"Squiffy," said Bill, "listen to me. We're pals, aren't we?"

"Absolutely. Bosom is the way I should put it."

"Very well, then. I want you to do me a great service."

"What?"

"Get my uncle out of the way to-night."

"Murder him?"

"If you like. Anyway, go to his room with him and see that he gets to sleep. To-night I want to be alone."

Lord Tidmouth had listened so far, but he refused to listen any further without lodging a definite protest. It was not so much the fact that, having been invited down to this place for a restful visit, he found himself requested by his host to go and tell his uncle bedtime stories; what was jarring his sensitive soul was the sinister atmosphere his old friend had begun to create.

"Bill, old man," he said, "you're being very mysterious this p.m. You shimmer about and dash in and out of rooms and make dark, significant speeches. All you need is a mask and false whiskers, and you could step into any mystery play and no questions asked. What's up?"

"I'll tell you."

"You forgot to say 'Hist!'"

Bill drew a chair up, and sank his voice to a whisper.

63

"I've got a big thing on to-night, and I must not be interrupted."

The pained look on Lord Tidmouth's face deepened. Of course, he supposed, it didn't really matter, seeing that they were alone, but he did wish that Bill could conduct a chat with an old crony without converting it into something that suggested an executive session of the " Black Hand " or a conference between apaches in some underground den in Montmartre.

" Old egg," he said, " do stop being mysterious. A big thing, you say? Well, tell me in a frank, manly way what it is. Get it right off your chest, and we'll both feel easier."

Bill mused, as if seeking words.

" Well, if you want the thing in a nutshell, to-night, Squiffy, I put my fate to the test—to win or lose it all, as the poet says."

" What poet?"

" What the devil does it matter what poet?"

" I merely asked."

" Montrose, if you really want to know."

" I don't."

Bill rose and resumed his pacing.

" Squiffy, do you know what it is to be in love?"

" Do I!" Lord Tidmouth spoke with a specialist's briskness. " My dear chap, except for an occasional rainy Monday, I don't suppose I've been out of love in the last six years. If you think a man can accumulate four wives without knowing what it is to be in love, try it and see."

" Well, I'm in love—so much in love that I could howl like a dog." He broke off and regarded his companion sharply. " I suppose," he said, " you're going to ask ' What dog?' "

" No, no," Lord Tidmouth assured him. He knew

64

—no man better—that there were all sorts of dogs: mastiffs, Pekes, Alsatians, Aberdeen terriers—scores of them. He had had no intention of saying 'What dog?'

Bill clenched his hands.

"It's awful! It's killing me!"

Lord Tidmouth was impressed.

"Bill, old man," he said, "this is serious news. We all thought you had got over it. So your old uncle was actually right! Well, well!"

"What do you mean?"

"I felt all along," proceeded Lord Tidmouth, "that something like this would happen. I wanted to warn you at the time. You see, having been married to her myself, I know her fascination. Yes, I nearly warned you at the time. 'Bill, old bird,' I came within a toucher of saying, 'pause before it is too late!' And now she's in a sanatorium, and you're pining for her. Oh, for the touch of a vanished hand——"

Bill stared an unfriendly stare.

"What on earth are you talking about? Who's in a sanatorium?"

"Lottie, of course."

"Lottie! Are you really idiot enough to suppose I'm in love with Lottie?"

His tone stung Lord Tidmouth.

"Better men than you have been, Bill," he said. "Myself, for one. The recent Higginbotham, presumably, for another. Let me tell you that there are many more difficult things in this world than falling in love with Lottie. Who are you in love with, then?"

Bill breathed rapturously.

"Sally!"

"Who's Sally?"

"Sally Smith."

Lord Tidmouth made a great mental effort.

"You don't mean the lady doctor down at Bingley?"

"Yes, I do."

"And you're in love with her?"

"Yes."

"Well," said Lord Tidmouth, bewildered, "this is all new stuff to me." He reflected. "But, if you miss her so much, why did you come down here, miles away from her?"

"I couldn't stay near her. It was driving me mad."

"Why?"

"She wouldn't let me tell her how much I loved her."

"I see."

Bill sprang up.

"Shall I tell you something, Squiffy?"

"By all means, old boy. I'm here to listen."

"I went to see her just before I left Bingley. I was absolutely determined that this time I would ask her to marry me. And do you know what happened?"

"What?"

A bitter laugh escaped Bill Bannister. At least Lord Tidmouth presumed that it was a bitter laugh. It had sounded more like a death-rattle.

"The moment I appeared—before I could even speak—she said, 'Put out your tongue!'"

"What did you do?"

"I put it out. 'Coated,' she said, and prescribed a mild tonic. Now, could I have followed that up by asking her to be my wife?"

"It wasn't what you would call a good cue," admitted Lord Tidmouth.

"I left," said Bill. "I came away, cursing—cursing everything: myself, my luck, and the fate that ever brought us together. I came down here, hoping that I would get over it. Not a chance. I'm worse than ever. But to-day, thank heaven, I got an idea."

"What was that?"

Bill looked about the room warily, as if suspecting the presence of Hugo Drakes in every nook and cranny. Relieved to see not even one, he resumed.

"I said to myself—she's a doctor. If I were ill, she would fly to my side. I looked her up in the telephone book. I found her name. I sat staring at that telephone book most of the afternoon, and it stared back at me. At five o'clock I gave in and . . ."

"Good Lord! Telephoned?"

"Yes. I pretended to be my man. I said that Mr. Bannister was seriously ill. We were sending the car and would she come at once."

Lord Tidmouth whistled.

"You certainly don't mind taking a chance."

"Not when there's something worth taking a chance for. It's two hours' ride in the car. The chauffeur left at half-past six. He should have reached her between half-past eight and nine. She ought to get here just about eleven."

"It's nearly eleven now."

"Yes. So can you wonder I'm a little jumpy?"

"Do you think she'll come?"

Bill quivered.

"She *must* come. She must. And I shall have it out with her, fairly and squarely. No more dodging and evasion. She shan't put me off this time. . . . So now perhaps you understand why you've got to keep my infernal, snooping, blundering, fussing busybody of an uncle out of the way."

" But he'll hear her drive up in the car."

" Why? A Rolls Royce doesn't make any noise."

Lord Tidmouth pondered.

" Well," he said at length, " I'm glad I'm not you."

" Why?"

" Because it is my firm and settled belief, old top, that, when she gets here and finds it was all a put-up job, this female is going to cut up rough."

" Don't call her a female."

" Well, she *is*, isn't she? I mean, that's rather what you might call the idea, I should have thought."

" She won't suspect. I shall convince her that I'm a sick man."

" By the time she has done with you, you probably will be. Hell hath no fury like a woman who's come eighty miles to be made a fool of."

" Don't be such a pessimist."

" Oh, all right. Have it your own way. All I can say is, may the Lord have mercy on your soul! I mean——"

" Sh!" whispered Bill sharply. He turned to the door. " Hullo, uncle. How's the putting coming along?"

Sir Hugo Drake was in a spacious mood. He beamed cordially.

" A very marked and sustained improvement."

" That's good. Off to bed now?"

" Yes, off to bed now. Early to bed, early to rise —nothing like it for keeping the eye clear and the hand steady."

" Tidmouth wants to come up with you and have a chat."

" Delighted."

" Tell him that excellent story of yours about the caddie and the india-rubber tee."

"Certainly. Well, come along, my boy. You coming, William?"

"No. I think I'll sit up a little longer."

"Good night, then. See you in the morning."

He wandered out. Lord Tidmouth lingered. He seemed a little anxious.

"Is that a long story, Bill?"

"Longish," admitted Bill. "But to help a pal, Squiffy——"

"Oh, all right," said Lord Tidmouth resignedly. "We Tidmouths never desert a friend. Well, honk-honk!"

He smiled bravely and followed Sir Hugo.

CHAPTER IX

THE summons to William Bannister's sick-bed had come to Sally, oddly enough, at a moment when she had just been thinking of that sufferer; for it is a curious fact that, busy woman though she was, she had found herself thinking quite a good deal about Bill in these last two weeks. And, if excuses must be made for her, let these meditations be set down to the quality in him that made him different from other men—his naïve directness.

Sally, both in her native America and during her stay in England, had been called upon at fairly frequent intervals to reject the proffered hands and hearts of many men. These had conducted the negotiations in a variety of ways, but none, not even the most forceful, had affected her quite like William Bannister. There was a childlike earnestness about his wooing which she found engaging.

It seemed a pity to her that with the admirable quality of directness he should combine that other quality which above all others in this world she despised and disliked—the quality of being content to sit down and loaf his life away on inherited money. She had seen so many of these good-looking, amiable, feckless Englishmen of private means, and all her instincts rose against them. Except as a joke, they were impossible. With so much to be done in life, they did nothing.

And Bill Bannister was one of them. She liked his looks and that easy, athletic swing of his body. She found him pleasant and agreeable. But he was also bone-idle, a well-bred waster, a drone who had nothing better to do with his time than hang about seashore resorts, dangling after perfumed and peroxided females of doubtful character.

For Sally's verdict on Lottie, pieced together from a brief acquaintance and a review of the dubious circumstances in which she had found her, was not a flattering one. She ignored the " Higginbotham ", which should have been such a hall-mark of respectability. She thoroughly disbelieved in the Higginbotham. Her views on the late Mr. Higginbotham were identical with those of Betsey Prig on her friend Sairey Gamp's friend Mrs. Harris. Firmly and decisively, Sally had set Lottie down in the ranks of those who are so well described as " no better than they should be ".

Sometimes Sally wondered a little why it was that she should feel this odd indignation against a woman who was virtually a complete stranger. It could not be because the other had ensnared William Bannister. William Bannister and his affairs were, of course, nothing to her. So what might have seemed to a superficial investigator a straight case of jealousy was nothing of the kind. It did not matter to her a row of pins who entrapped William Bannister.

Nevertheless, every time she thought of Lottie an odd thrill of indignation passed through Sally.

And every time she thought of William Bannister wasting his time on such a woman she felt another thrill of indignation.

The whole thing was perplexing.

Her feelings, as she bowled along the Hampshire roads in Bill's Rolls Royce to-night, were mixed. She was sorry he was not feeling well, though she much doubted whether his ailment was as severe as she had been given to understand. Men were all alike—men of Bill Bannister's kind especially so. A pain in the toe and they thought they were dying.

Of the chance of visiting the home of Bill's ancestors she was glad. With her American love of the practical she combined that other American love for old houses and their historic associations. She had read up the Manor, Woollam Chersey, in *Stately Homes of England*, and was intrigued to find that parts of it dated back to the thirteenth century, while even the more modern portions were at least Elizabethan. She looked forward to seeing on the morrow its park, its messuages, its pleasances, and the record-breaking oak planted by the actual hand of King Charles the First.

To-night, as she passed through the great gateway and bowled up the drive, there was little to be seen. Dark trees and banks of shrubs blocked what little would have been visible in the darkness. It was only when the car stopped that she realized that she had reached the house.

Sally got out and dismissed the chauffeur. She could find her way in. There was an open french window at the end of the lawn on her left, from which light proceeded. She made her way thither, and on the threshold stopped. A rather remarkable sight met her eyes. Inside, walking with the brisk step of a man in perfect health up and down a cosily furnished room, was her patient. Anyone less wasted with sickness she had never seen.

Up and down the floor paced Bill. He was smoking a cigarette. A thrill of honest indignation shot through Sally. She saw all. And in the darkness her teeth came together with a little click.

Somewhere in the room a telephone tinkled. Bill moved beyond her range of vision, but his voice came to her clearly.

"Hullo? . . . Grosvenor 7525? Doctor Smith's house? . . . This is Mr. Bannister's valet speaking. Can you tell me if the doctor has left? . . . Just before nine? . . . Thank you. . . . Hullo. . . . The doctor will not be returning to-night. . . . Yes, very serious. She will have to sit up with the patient. . . . Yes. . . . Good night."

There came the click of the receiver being replaced, and then for some moments silence. But a few moments later there was something for Sally to see again. Her patient had apparently left the room during this interval, for he now reappeared wearing a dark silk dressing-gown. He then proceeded to arrange a pillow and lie down on the sofa. And after that he seemed to be of the opinion that the stage was adequately set, for he remained there without moving.

Sally waited no longer. Outwardly calm, but seething within with what Lord Tidmouth had called the fury of a woman who has driven eighty miles to be made a fool of, she walked briskly into the room.

"Good evening!" she said, suddenly and sharply, and Bill Bannister shot up from the sofa as though propelled by an explosive.

CHAPTER X

BILL stood staring. His nervous system, in its highly-strung condition, was not proof against this entirely unexpected greeting. The Manor was not haunted, but if it had been and if the family spectre had suddenly presented itself at his elbow and barked at him, he would have reacted in a very similar way. He gulped, and fingered his collar.

" You made me jump! " he said plaintively.

Sally was cool and hostile.

" Weren't you expecting me? "

" Er—yes. Yes. Of course. "

" Well, here I am. "

This was undeniable, and Bill should have accepted it as such. He should also have sunk back on the sofa, thus indicating that the effort he had just made had been too much for his frail strength. Instead, he became gushingly hospitable.

" I say, do sit down, won't you? Won't you have something to eat—something to drink? "

Sally raised her eyebrows.

" I must say, " she observed, " that for a man who has brought a doctor a night journey of eighty miles you look surprisingly well. "

Bill rejected the idea passionately.

" I'm not, " he cried. " I'm desperately ill. "

" Oh! " said Sally.

Bill's manner became defiant, almost sullen.

" You can't tell how a man's feeling just by looking at him, " he said.

" I don't intend to. We'll have a thorough examination. "

A devout look came into Bill's eyes.

" It's like a dream," he said.

" What is?"

" Your being here—in my home——"

" Tell me your symptoms," said Sally.

Bill blinked.

" Did you say symptoms?"

" I did."

" Well—I say, do let me help you off with your coat."

" I can manage," said Sally. She removed her wraps and threw them on a chair. " Now, then. . . . Hello! You're shivering!"

" Am I?" said Bill.

" Do you feel chilly?"

" No. Hot all over."

" Let me feel your pulse. . . . H'm! A hundred and ten. Very interesting. And yet you haven't a temperature. A pulse of a hundred and ten without fever. Quite remarkable. Do you feel dizzy?"

" Yes," said Bill truthfully.

" Then sit down."

" Thanks," said Bill, doing so. " Won't you?"

Sally opened her bag, and from it removed an odd something at which her patient gazed with unconcealed apprehension.

" What's that?" he asked.

" Stethoscope," said Sally briefly. " Now we can get on."

" Yes," said Bill doubtfully. He had heard of stethoscopes, and knew them to be comparatively harmless, but he was still uneasy. In his visions of this moment he had always seen this girl bending over him with a divine sympathy in her lovely eyes —trembling a little, perhaps—possibly passing a cool

75

hand over his forehead. Up to the present she had done none of these things. Instead, she seemed to him—though this, he forced himself to feel, was merely due to his guilty conscience—annoyed about something.

A simple solution of the mystery came to him. In spite of the fact that she had ignored his previous offer of refreshment, she really needed some. She had had a tiring journey, and tiring journeys always affected women like this. He recalled an aunt of his who, until you shot a cup of tea into her, always became —even after the simplest trip—a menace to man and beast.

"I say, do have something to eat and drink," he urged.

Sally frowned.

"Later," she said. "Now, then, the symptoms, please."

Bill made a last effort to stem the tide.

"Must we talk about my symptoms?" he asked plaintively.

"Might I mention," retorted Sally, "that I've driven eighty miles simply in order to talk about them?"

"But surely there's not such a desperate hurry as all that? I mean, can't we have just five minutes' conversation——" Her eye was not encouraging, but he persevered. "You don't seem to understand how tremendously happy it makes me to see you sitting there——"

Sally cut into his rambling discourse like an east wind.

"It may seem eccentric to you, Mr. Bannister," she said frigidly, "but when I get an urgent call to visit an invalid I find my thoughts sort of straying in the direction of his health. It's a foolish habit we doctors have. So may I repeat—the symptoms?" She fixed him with a compelling glance. "When," she asked, "did you first notice that there was anything wrong with you?"

Bill could answer that.

"Three weeks ago."

"About the time you first met me?"

"Yes."

"An odd coincidence. What happened?"

"My heart stood still."

"It couldn't."

"It did."

"Hearts don't stand still."

"Mine did," insisted Bill stoutly. "It then had strong palpitations. They've been getting worse ever since. Sometimes," he proceeded, beginning to get into his stride, "I feel as if I were going to suffocate. It is as if I were being choked inside by an iron hand."

"Probably dyspepsia. Go on."

"My hands tremble. My head aches. My feet feel like lead. I have floating spots before the eyes, and I can't sleep."

"No?"

"Not a wink. I toss on my pillow. I turn feverishly from side to side. But it's all no good. Dawn comes and finds me still awake. I stare before me hopelessly. Another night," concluded Bill with fine pathos, "has passed, and in the garden outside the roosters are crowing."

"Anything connected with roosters," said Sally, "you had better tell to a vet."

A man in a sitting position finds it difficult to draw himself up indignantly, but Bill did his best.

"Is that all you can do to a patient—laugh at him?"

"If you think I am finding this a laughing matter," said Sally grimly, "you're wrong. Undress, please," she added casually.

Bill started violently.

"What—what did you say?" he quavered.

"Undress."

"But—but I can't."

"Would you like me to help you?"

"I mean—is it necessary?"

"Quite."

"But——"

Sally surveyed him coolly.

"I notice the vascular motors are still under poor control," she said. "Why do you blush?"

"What do you expect me to do—cheer?" Bill's voice shook. The prude in him had been deeply stirred. "Look here," he demanded, "do you mean to tell me this is the first time any of your male patients has jibbed at undressing in front of you?"

"Oh, no! I had a case last week."

"I'm glad," said Bill primly, "that somebody has a little delicacy beside myself."

"It wasn't delicacy. He didn't want me to see that he was wearing detachable cuffs. You know the kind ? They fasten on with a clip, and are generally made of celluloid—like motion-picture films."

"Er—do you go much to the pictures?" asked Bill.

Sally refused to allow the conversation to be diverted.

"Never mind whether I go to the pictures," she said. "Please undress."

Bill gave up the struggle. He threw off his dressing-gown.

"That'll do for the present," said Sally. "I can't think what you were making such a fuss about. Your cuffs aren't detachable. . . . Now, please."

She placed the stethoscope against his chest and applied her ear to it. Bill gazed down upon the top of her head emotionally.

"I wonder," he said, "if you realize what this means to me—to see you here—in my home—to feel that we two are alone together at last——"

"Did you ever have any children's disease?"

"No! . . . Alone together at last——"

"Mumps?" said Sally.

Bill gulped.

"No!"

"Measles?"

"No!" shouted Bill.

Sally looked up.

"I merely asked," she said.

Bill was quivering with self-pity.

"It's too bad," he said. "Here I am, trying to pour out my soul to you, and you keep interrupting with questions about mumps and measles."

"My dear Mr. Bannister," said Sally, "I'm not interested in your soul. My job has to do with what the hymn-book calls your ' vile body '."

There was a pause. She put her ear to the stethoscope again.

"Can't you understand," cried Bill, breaking into eloquence once more, "that the mere sight of you sets every nerve in my body tingling? When you came in I felt like a traveller in the desert who is dying of thirst and suddenly comes upon an oasis. I felt——"

"And retching or nausea?"

"Oh, my God!"

"Now tell me about your sex-life," said Sally.

Bill recoiled.

"Stand still."

"I won't stand still," said Bill explosively.

"Then move about," said Sally equably. "But give me the information I asked for."

Bill eyed her austerely.

"Don't you know the meaning of the word "reticence"?" he asked.

"Of course not. I'm a doctor."

Bill took a turn up and down the room.

"Well, naturally," he said with dignity, halting once more, "I have had—er—experiences—like other men."

Sally was at the stethoscope again.

"Um-hum," she said.

"I admit it. There *have* been women in my life."

"Say ninety-nine."

"Not half as many as that!" cried Bill, starting.

"Say ninety-nine, please."

"Oh!" Bill became calmer. "I didn't—I thought I imagined that you were referring—— Well, in short, ninety-nine."

Sally straightened herself. She put the stethoscope away.

"Thank you," she said. "Your lungs appear to be all right. Remove the rest of your clothes, please."

"What!"

"You heard."

"I won't do it!" cried Bill, pinkly.

Sally shrugged her shoulders.

"Just as you like," she said. "Then the examination is finished." She paused. "Tell me, Mr. Bannister," she asked, "just to satisfy my curiosity, what sort of a fool did you think I was?"

Bill gaped.

"I beg your pardon?"

"I'm glad you have the grace to. Did you imagine

that this was the first time I had ever been called out into the country?''

'' I——''

'' Let me tell you it is not. And do you know what usually happens when I am called to the country? I see you don't,'' she said, as Bill choked wordlessly. '' Well, when I am sent for to visit a patient in the country, Mr. Bannister, the road is lined with anxious relatives waiting for the car. They help me out and bustle me into the house. They run around like chickens with their heads cut off, and everybody who isn't having hysterics on the stairs is in the kitchen brewing camomile tea.''

'' Camomile tea?''

'' People who get sick in the country are always given camomile tea.''

'' I never knew that before.''

'' You'll learn a lot of things,'' said Sally, '' if you stick around with me. And one of them, Mr. Bannister, is that I'm not a complete idiot. You'll excuse my slight warmth. I've driven eighty miles on a fool's errand, and somehow I find it a little irritating.''

Bill waved his hands agitatedly.

'' But I tell you you're wrong!''

'' What! Have you the nerve to pretend there's anything whatever the matter with you?''

'' Certainly there is. I—I'm not myself.''

'' I congratulate you.''

'' I'm a very sick man.''

'' And I'm a very angry woman.''

Bill coughed an injured cough.

'' Of course, if you don't believe me, there's nothing more to say.''

'' Oh, isn't there?'' said Sally. '' I'll find plenty more to say, trust *me*. I may as well tell you, Mr.

Bannister, that when I arrived I looked in at the window and saw you striding about, the picture of health. A moment later the telephone rang, and you went to it and said you were your valet——''

Bill flushed darkly. He moved to the window and stood there looking out, with his back turned. Sally watched him with satisfaction. Her outburst had left her feeling more amiable.

Bill wheeled round. His face was set. He spoke through clenched teeth.

'' I see,'' he said. '' So you knew all along, and you've been amusing yourself at my expense?''

'' You might say, getting a little of my own back.''

'' You've had a lot of fun with me, haven't you?''

'' Quite a good deal, since you mention it.''

'' And now, I suppose, you're going?''

'' Going?'' said Sally. '' Of course I'm not. I shall sleep here. You don't expect me to drive all night, do you?''

'' I beg your pardon,'' said Bill. He pointed to the gallery that ran round two sides of the room. '' You'll be up there.''

'' Thank you.''

Bill laughed shortly.

'' Well, it's something, I suppose, that you have consented to sleep under my roof.''

'' You could hardly have expected me to go to the garage.''

'' No. I suppose you would like to be turning in, then?''

'' Yes, please.''

'' I'll show you your room.''

'' You have already.''

'' Well . . . good night,'' said Bill.

'' Good night,'' said Sally.

He stood without moving, watching her as she went up the stairs. She reached the door, opened it, and was gone. Bill turned sharply and flung himself into a chair.

He had been sitting for some minutes, with only his thoughts for unpleasant company, when there was the sound of a footstep on the stairs, and he sprang up as though electrified.

But it was not Sally. It was only Lord Tidmouth. That ill-used gentleman was looking rather weary, and his eye, as he reached the foot of the stairs, was fixed purposefully on the decanter on the table. He moved towards it with a stealthy rapidity, like a leopard; and only when he had poured into a glass a generous measure of the life-restoring fluid did he turn to his host.

CHAPTER XI

"HULLO, Bill, old man," said his lordship.

Bill regarded him sourly.

"Oh, it's you, is it?" he said.

Lord Tidmouth sighed.

"What's left of me after an hour's *tête-à-tête* with the old relative," he said. "Bill, that uncle of yours waggles a wicked jawbone!"

"Does he?"

"He talked and talked and talked. And then he talked some more. Mostly about his mashie-shots. I got him off to bye-bye at last, and I've tottered down to restore the tissues with a spot of alcohol. They say," continued Lord Tidmouth earnestly, "that strong drink biteth like a serpent and—if I remember correctly—stingeth like a jolly old adder. Well, all I have to say is—let it! That's what I say, Bill— *let* it! It's what it's there for. Excuse me for a moment, old man, while I mix myself a stiffish serpent-and-soda."

He turned to the table again.

"So you got him off to sleep?" said Bill.

Lord Tidmouth's fingers had been closing about the siphon, but he courteously suspended operations in order to reply to his host's question.

"Yes," he said, "I got him off to sleep. But at infinite cost to life and limb. I feel a perfect wreck. However, I've left him slumbering like a little child, one hand still clutching James Braid's *Advanced Golf*. So that's that."

"Much obliged. Well, I'll be turning in."

"Half a moment," said Lord Tidmouth. "Isn't

it about time that lady doctor of yours rolled up? Allowing two hours for the journey—that is, assuming she had no puncture, or blow-out, or engine trouble, or lost the way, or——"

"Oh, go to blazes!" said Bill.

Lord Tidmouth watched his disappearing back with rather an aggrieved air.

"Not one of our good listeners!" he murmured.

Then, having sterner work before him than the consideration of a host's brusqueness, he addressed himself once more to the siphon.

Lord Tidmouth was a careful man with siphons. Experience had taught him that a too vehement pressing of the trigger led to disaster. Strong drink might bite like an adder, but soda-water could spout like a geyser. He knew the perils perfectly, and it was, therefore, all the more annoying that a moment later a hissing stream should have shot up between his cuff and his skin.

This happened because, as he was in the very act of working the trigger arrangement, a loud and breezy voice in his immediate rear spoke.

Voices speaking to Lord Tidmouth where no voice should have been always affected him powerfully. He became involved in a Niagara of seltzer, from which he emerged to gaze censoriously at the intruder.

"If you know me a thousand years," he was beginning, as he turned, "never do that again!" Then he saw the new-comer steadily and saw her whole. For it was a She. It was, as a matter of fact, none other than the first of his battalion of wives—the exuberant Lottie Higginbotham. And he stared at her as at a vision.

"Great God of Battles!" said Lord Tidmouth. "You!"

Lottie was completely at her ease. She placed on the floor the suit-case which she was carrying, and with a dexterous hand removed the whisky-and-soda from her companion's grasp. She drank deeply, and, having done so, sighed with satisfaction.

" You always did know how to mix them, Squiffy," she said.

It was a handsome compliment—and rather touching, in its way, as giving evidence that the memory of the dear old days still lingered—but Lord Tidmouth paid no attention to it. He was still goggling.

" What on earth are you doing here?" he asked blankly.

" Who, me?" said Lottie.

" Yes, you."

" I was sent for."

" How do you mean, sent for?"

" I got a telegram from Bill's uncle asking me to come."

A blinding flash of light illumined Lord Tidmouth's darkness. He recalled the veiled hints the old boy had dropped earlier in the evening. So this was what he had been hinting at.

" Did he specify that you were to come beetling in at midnight?" he inquired.

" I came directly I got the telegram. It sounded interesting."

" Oh!" Lord Tidmouth pondered for a while. " Well, welcome to the Manor, and all that sort of rot," he said.

Lottie was very bright and animated. She flitted about the room like a humming-bird.

" This looks a pretty good sort of place," she said. " I can see myself in a place like this. Who are all these?" she asked, indicating the portraits.

"Just ancestors," said Lord Tidmouth. "Bill's ancestors."

"No beauty-chorus," was Lottie's comment, after she had made her round of inspection. "Talking of Bill, is he expecting me?"

"No, he's not!"

"Oh, then, I shall come on him as a surprise."

"Surprise," said Lord Tidmouth, with feeling, "is *right*."

"Listen," said Lottie. "Do you know why Sir Hugo wanted me to come here?"

Lord Tidmouth was embarrassed. He did know, but he could hardly impart the information.

"I couldn't tell you."

"I'm telling *you*," said Lottie brightly. "I thought it all out on the train. Bill has discovered that he can't get on without me. I knew it would happen. He's pining for me. Yessir, that's what that boy's doing—pining for me."

"Well——"

"It stands to reason," argued Lottie, "he must be pretty crazy about me to make his old uncle wire for me in such a hurry."

Lord Tidmouth closed his eyes. He seemed to be praying.

"Full information," he said, "will no doubt be supplied to-morrow by the aged relative. But, if you'll take a pal's advice—if you'll be guided by one to whom you once stood in a sacred and tender relationship—viz. marriage," explained Lord Tidmouth, "you will biff off at the earliest opportunity."

"What!"

"At the very earliest opp."

"What are you talking about?"

Lord Tidmouth groaned in spirit. He was feeling

87

unequal to the situation. At any moment now, he told himself, that lady doctor of old Bill's would be breezing in, and naturally the last thing the dear old boy would wish was to have the place congested with extraneous females. Sir Hugo Drake, the pre-eminent dodderer, had made a proper mess of things.

"You just tuck yourself away somewhere till to-morrow morning," he urged, "and then we'll smuggle you off."

Lottie stared. She had never had a very high opinion of her former husband's intelligence, but she had never known him descend into such abysses of lunacy as this.

"I think you're cuckoo," she said. "What do I want to go away for? Bill's in love with me and can't live without me."

"Absolutely," said Lord Tidmouth. "Of course. Quite so. Yes. Beyond a question. Indubitably. Only——"

"Well?"

"Nothing, nothing. You see that room on top of the stairs? Technically, it's mine, but you can have it for to-night. Not the one on the right—that's Bill's. The one on the left. Accept it with my hearty good wishes."

"What'll you do?"

"Oh, I'll doze somewhere. And in the morn-ing——"

Lottie eyed him sharply.

"Listen," she said.

"Hullo?"

"Is anything the matter?"

"The matter?"

"You're acting sort of mysterious, it seems to me, and I'm wondering if there's any funny business going on. Are you trying to keep Bill and me apart?"

"No, no."

"Well, you better hadn't, that's all," said Lottie decidedly. "If I find you're pulling any smooth stuff, I'll murder you. Nothing could be fairer than that, could it?"

"Absolutely not."

"Well, good night then."

"Good night," said Lord Tidmouth.

Alone at last, he found in the confused welter of his thoughts one thing clear—that he had not yet had that drink and that he wanted it now more than ever. He moved to the table and began the ritual again. He had barely completed it when once more a voice spoke behind him.

"You still up?" It was his old friend Bill Bannister. There was surprise in Bill's voice; also irritation and peevishness. "Why the devil don't you go to bed?"

"Why don't you?" rejoined Lord Tidmouth, not unreasonably.

"I'm restless," said Bill. "I can't sleep."

Lord Tidmouth eyed him pityingly. The non-sleeping his old friend had done so far would, he felt, be a mere nothing compared to the non-sleeping he would do when he heard the latest.

"Bill," he said, and his tone was the unmistakable tone of a man who is going to break something gently, "I've a piece of information to impart."

"Keep it for the morning."

"But it's serious. Bill, we have a little visitor."

"I know. I know."

Lord Tidmouth was relieved.

"Oh, you *know*. I thought you didn't. But how

do you know?" he went on, puzzled. "She only just——"

"Stop babbling and go to bed."

"Yes, but, Bill——"

"Shut up."

"Lottie——"

"Don't talk to me about Lottie."

"I was only saying that Lottie——"

"Stop it!"

"I just wanted to mention that Lottie——"

"Will you get out?"

Lord Tidmouth gave it up.

"Oh, all right," he said resignedly. "I think I'll take a stroll in the garden. Well, bung-oh. And I came down here for a rest-cure."

CHAPTER XII

BILL ran quickly up the stairs and knocked at Sally's door. The conclusion of their recent conversation had left him in a nervous and disordered frame of mind. Though she had plainly shown herself of the opinion that all had been said that needed to be said, he was unable to adopt this view. He was full of talk, and considered that in their late interview he had but scratched the surface.

"Sally," he said in a choking voice.

A voice from within answered:

"What is it? Who's there?"

"Come out. I want to talk to you."

Sally emerged. She was wearing a pale green wrap.

"Well?" she said.

Bill did not answer immediately. The sight of the wrap had had a stunning effect. He had not supposed that it was possible that this girl could look prettier than when he had seen her last, but she had accomplished this stupendous feat with ease. His legs shook, and he leaned against the banisters.

"Have you got everything you want?" he managed to ask at length.

"Yes, thank you. I find that you have given me your room."

"Yes."

"Where are you going to sleep?"

"I shall manage."

"Oh? Well, it's very kind of you." She paused. "Was that all you wanted to say to me?"

"No," said Bill urgently.

"Well?"

"Don't stand in that doorway. Come out here."

"Just as you like. Well?"

Bill gulped.

"I've been walking about in the garden," he said.

"Yes?"

"Thinking."

"Yes?"

"Trying to get a grip on myself."

"I hope you were successful," said Sally politely.

"I wasn't."

Sally smiled indulgently.

"Too bad," she said. "Well, good night."

"Come back."

"Sorry," said Sally, returning. "I thought you had finished."

"I haven't begun." He moved to the head of the stairs. "Come on down. We can't talk here."

"Do we want to talk?"

"I do."

"Oh, very well."

She followed him down the stairs.

"Now," said Bill, "we can begin."

Sally had perched herself on the arm of a chair. She eyed him coolly.

"Don't you country-folk ever go to bed?" she asked. "I had no idea you wandered about the house all night, knocking at people's doors and dragging them out for cosy talks."

Bill scowled.

"You seem amused."

"I am," said Sally.

"Oh, well, let me tell you," said Bill, "that we have now finished with the amusing part of this business. I now propose to call your attention to the fact that this little farce, which seems to entertain you

so much, has a serious side. I'm going to have it out
with you here and now."

" Proceed. You interest me strangely."

" Don't laugh at me!"

" What else do you expect me to do?"

Bill ground his heel into the carpet.

" In the first place," he said, " I admit that I did
get you down here by a trick."

" A contemptible trick."

" That's as it may be. Anyway, you're here, and
you've got to listen to me."

" And to cut a long story short——"

" I'll make it short enough. Three words will be
sufficient. I love you."

" This is wonderful news."

" That's right—laugh! Listen. You think you
can play the fool with a man as much as you please
—hold him off with a raised eyebrow when he be-
comes too pressing—keep him under control with a
laugh——"

" Why, this is eloquence! The boy orator!"

" Oh, you may sneer, but you know in your heart
you're afraid."

Sally stiffened. The smile faded from her lips.
She froze.

" Afraid? You flatter yourself."

" I may not be your match at fencing," said Bill,
" but the bludgeon is quite as handy a weapon as the
rapier."

" From the insight you have given me into your
character, I should have thought your favourite
weapon would have been the black-jack."

" You and I are going to settle things to-night. You
have known right from the start that I loved you, and
from our first meeting you have fought me. All

right! To-night shall decide which of us two is the strongest."

"*Stronger*. Didn't they teach you that at school? Even when insulting a woman, always be grammatical."

Bill glowered.

"So I'm insulting you? By offering you my love?"

"No," said Sally. "By suggesting that, if I refuse it, you will employ force. For that is what you are suggesting, is it not?"

"Yes, it is."

"Good!" said Sally. "Then excuse me for a moment."

She got up.

"What are you doing?"

"I was merely going to fetch my bag and prepare a soothing injection. I should think two centigrams of morphia would be sufficient."

Bill seized her wrist.

"Stop fooling!"

"Oh!" Sally could not restrain a gasp. "You're very strong."

"I'm glad you're beginning to realize it."

"Let me go."

"I won't!" said Bill. "Never again. Well," he said, "here you are in my arms. How do you like it? Now try to be aloof and superior; now try to hold me off with your matter-of-factness."

"You beast!"

"Beast, eh?" Bill laughed. "I'm improving. Just now I was only a poor fool—just something to laugh at. Laugh at me now—if you can."

Sally suddenly ceased to struggle.

"Oh, well," she said, "they always warned me it was dangerous to be a doctor. Do you know, the last man who treated me like this was a lunatic, in the violent ward of an asylum. But he was more decent than you. He merely wanted to murder me."

She felt the arms that were holding her unclasp. She sank on to the sofa. Bill was looking away from her, out of the window. After a moment he spoke.

"All right," he said. "You win. I beg your pardon," he said formally.

Sally was herself again.

"Don't mention it," she said. "You might just as well apologize for having rheumatism."

"What?"

"It wasn't your fault. The thing was purely pathological. But I shall have to cure you. . . . I'll write you a little prescription."

Bill started.

"For God's sake!"

Sally went to the desk, and took up a pencil.

"Kalii bromati," he heard her murmur. "Natrii bromatii. . . . Grammata quinque. . . ." She got up. "Here you are," she said amiably. "One powder three times a day after meals. Any druggist will make that up for you."

"You're very kind."

"In addition there will be hygienic regulation of your mode of living. Avoid excitement and mental strain."

"Thanks!" said Bill. "That's a great help."

"Take plenty of fresh air, do physical jerks every morning, and eat plenty of vegetables. Good night!"

She stroked his face softly, and he quivered. He looked up amazed.

"Sally!"

"What's the matter?"

"You stroked my face!"

" Yes."

" Gently."

" Yes."

" Almost—lovingly."

" Yes."

Bill blinked.

" Then——"

" Oh, don't jump to conclusions," said Sally. " The gesture was purely automatic. We doctors often stroke our patients' faces when they have passed the crisis."

" Oh! So you think I have passed the crisis?"

" I think so. You see, you had the sense to call in a good doctor. Good night."

She walked composedly up the stairs. And, as she did so, the door of Lottie's room opened, and its occupant came yawning into view.

" Squiffy!" called Lottie, who, thinking things over in bed, had decided that what was needed to induce sleep was another of her erstwhile mate's scientifically blended glassfuls.

Her eye fell on Bill, gaping below, and she gave tongue cheerily.

" Hullo, Bill!"

She perceived Sally.

" Hul-lo!" she said.

Sally said nothing. She walked into her room; and Bill, standing as in a trance, heard the key click in the lock.

Bill came to life. Dashing past Lottie, he rushed at the door. He shook the handle.

" Sally!" he cried. " Sally!"

There was no answer.

CHAPTER XIII

SIR HUGO DRAKE had passed a restful night, undisturbed by dreams of foozled mashie-shots. Morning found him sleeping like the little child of Lord Tidmouth's description. Waking as the sun crept over his pillow, he yawned, sat up, and perceived that another day, with all its possibilities for improving a man's putting, had arrived. He donned his favourite suit of plus-fours, and, taking putter and ball, went down to the hall.

He had just grounded the ball and was taking careful aim at the leg of the sofa, when from the recesses of that sofa two clenched fists suddenly rose in the air and an unseen someone uttered the gasping sigh of the newly awakened.

" God bless my soul!" said Sir Hugo.

It was his nephew William. That much was plain from the tousled head which now appeared. Sir Hugo drew nearer to observe this strange phenomenon.

" Oh, hullo, uncle," said Bill drowsily.

Sir Hugo was a man who always went to the root of a problem.

" William," he cried, " what are you doing there?"

" Eugh!" replied Bill, stretching. He blinked. " What?" he asked sleepily.

Sir Hugo was not to be diverted from his theme.

" That's what *I* said—' What?' "

" What?"

" Yes, what?"

Bill rubbed his eyes.

" What what?" he asked.

Sir Hugo became impatient.

"Good God, boy, wake up!"

Bill rose to his feet. He inspected his uncle uncertainly.

"What did you ask me?" he said.

"Have you been sleeping there all night?"

"Yes," said Bill. "Oo, I'm stiff!"

"But why?"

"Well, wouldn't *you* be stiff if you had slept all night on a hardish sofa?"

"I'm not asking you why you're stiff. I'm asking why you slept on that sofa?"

Bill was awake now.

"I gave up my room to a lady. Yes, I—— Oh, heavens!" said Bill peevishly. "Need we do this vaudeville cross-talk stuff so early in the morning?"

"But I don't understand. Did a lady arrive last night?"

"Yes. Soon after eleven."

"Good God!" Like Lord Tidmouth, he felt that Lottie had not wasted time. "Did you see her?"

"Of course I saw her."

"I mean, you spoke to her? You had a talk—a conversation—an interview with her?"

"Yes."

Sir Hugo probed delicately for information.

"What occurred?"

"How do you mean, what occurred?"

"Well—er—did you come to an understanding?"

"No!" said Bill.

"Did you—ah, how shall I put it?—did you shower her face with kisses?"

"No, I did not!"

Sir Hugo looked like a minor prophet receiving good news about the latest battle with the Philistines.

"Capital! Excellent! Precisely as I foresaw.

When the test came, you found you were a Bannister, after all. I knew it. I knew it."

Bill regarded his rejoicing relative sourly.

"Uncle," he said, "you're gibbering."

He spoke with feeling. The one thing a man does not want to meet, when he has slept all night on a sofa and has not had breakfast, is a gibbering uncle.

"I am not gibbering," said Sir Hugo. "I repeat that you have proved yourself a true Bannister. You have come nobly out of the ordeal. I foresaw the whole thing. Directly you saw this woman in the home of your ancestors, beneath the gaze of the family portraits, the scales fell from your eyes and your infatuation withered and died."

Bill would have none of this.

"It did not wither," he said emphatically.

Sir Hugo stared.

"It did not wither?"

"It did not wither!"

"You say it did not wither?"

Bill gave him a nasty look.

"Damn it, uncle, you're back to the cross-talk stuff again."

"You mean to tell me," cried Sir Hugo, "that, even after you have seen this woman in your ancestral home, you are still infatuated with her?"

"More than ever."

"Good God!"

"And I'm not going to rest," said Bill, "till I have made her my wife."

"Your wife?"

"My wife."

"Your——"

Bill held up a warning hand.

"Uncle!"

"You want to *marry* her?"

"Yes."

"But—— Good heavens, boy! Have you re-flected?"

"Yes."

"Have you considered?"

"Yes."

"Have you gone off your head?"

"Yes. No," said Bill quickly. "What do you mean?"

"You—a Bannister—want to marry this woman?"

"Yes. And I'm going to find her now and tell her so."

Sir Hugo gazed after him blankly. He mopped his forehead and stared gloomily into the future. He was feeling that this was going to put him right off his game. He doubted if he would break a hundred to-day —after this.

He was still brooding bleakly on this lamentable state of affairs when the door of the room to the left of the stairs opened and Lottie came out, all brightness and camaraderie. Her air of sparkling-eyed cheerfulness smote Sir Hugo like a blow, even before she had come within speaking range.

"Hello, Doc," said Lottie amiably.

"Good morning," said Sir Hugo.

"You don't seem surprised to see me."

"No. I heard that you had arrived. I have just been talking to William, and he has told me the appalling news."

Lottie was puzzled.

"What news?"

"He is resolved to marry you."

A slight but distinct cloud marred Lottie's shining morning face. She looked at her companion narrowly, and her hands began to steal towards her hips.

"Just what," she asked, "do you mean by 'appalling news'?"

"It is appalling," said Sir Hugo stoutly.

Lottie breathed softly through her nose.

"You think I'm not good enough for him?"

"Precisely."

"Listen!" said Lottie, in a spirit of inquiry. "What's the earliest in the morning you ever got a sock right on the side of the head?"

Sir Hugo became aware that something he had said —he could not think what—had apparently disturbed and annoyed this woman before him. He did not like the way she was advancing upon him. He had seen tigresses in the Zoo walk just like that.

A swift thinker, he took refuge behind a chair and held up a deprecating hand.

"Now, now, my good girl——"

"Don't you call me a good girl!"

"No, no," said Sir Hugo hastily. "You're not. You're not. But, my dear Miss——"

"Mrs."

"My dear Mrs.——"

"Higginbotham is the name."

"My dear Mrs. Higginbotham, cannot you see for yourself how utterly impossible this match is?"

Lottie drew in her breath sharply.

"Honest," she said, "I owe it to my womanly feelings to paste you one."

"No, no. Be reasonable."

"How do you mean it's impossible?" demanded Lottie warmly. "If Bill's so crazy about me——"

"But William is a Bannister."

"What of it?"

" And you——" Sir Hugo carefully paused. He realized that infinite tact was required. " After all —in the kindliest spirit of academic inquiry—who *are* you?"

" *Née* Burke. Relict of the late Edwin Higginbotham," said Lottie briefly.

" I mean, what is your family?"

" If anybody's been telling you I've a family, it's not true."

" You misunderstand me. But the whole thing is impossible—quite impossible."

" How do you mean?"

" My dear young lady," said Sir Hugo, " have you really reflected what marriage to William would be like? My nephew, you must remember, my dear Mrs. Higginbotham, is a Bannister. And, without meaning to be in any way offensive, I think you will admit that your social position is scarcely equal to that of a Bannister. I fear the county would resent it bitterly if William should be considered to have married beneath him. Cannot you see how unpleasant it would be for you—received by nobody, ignored by all? Your proud, generous spirit would never endure it. And, believe me," said Sir Hugo feelingly, " this damn out-of-the-way place is quite dull enough even when you have got a neighbour or two to talk to. My dear girl, you would be bored stiff in a week."

Lottie frowned thoughtfully. Hers was a mind that could face facts, and she had to admit that she had never considered this aspect of the matter before.

" I never thought of that," she said.

" Think of it now," urged Sir Hugo. " Think of it very carefully. In fact, in order to enable you to think the better, I will leave you. Just sit quietly in one of these chairs, and try to picture to yourself what

102

it would be like for you here during—say—the months of January and February, with no amusements, no friends—in short, nothing to entertain you but William. Think it over, Mrs. Higginbotham,'' said Sir Hugo, '' and if you wish to secure me for a further consultation you will find me walking in the raspberry bushes.''

He bustled out, and Lottie, taking his advice, sat down in a chair and began to think. He had opened up a new line of thought.

Presently there was a sound behind her—the sound of one meditatively singing '' I Fear no Foe in Shining Armour '', and she was aware that she had been joined by Lord Tidmouth.

'' Hullo, old egg!'' said Lord Tidmouth.

'' Hullo, Squiffy!'' said Lottie.

She was pleased to see him. Although, some years earlier, she had been compelled to sever the matrimonial bond that linked them, she had always thought kindly of dear old Squiffy. He was her sort. He liked dancing and noisy parties and going to the races and breezing to and fro about London. Theirs, in short, was a spiritual affinity.

'' Squiffy,'' she said, '' I've just been having a talk with old what's-his-name.''

'' Sir Hugo?''

'' Yes. Do you know what he said?''

'' I can tell you *verbatim*,'' replied Lord Tidmouth confidently. '' He said that, while fair off the tee, he had a lot of trouble with his mashie-shots, and this he attributed to——''

'' No. He was talking about Bill.''

'' What about Bill?''

'' Well, what would happen if I married Bill.''

'' What did the old boy predict?''

'' He said I would be bored stiff.''

Lord Tidmouth considered.

"Well," he said, "I'm not saying he wasn't right. Bill is a stout fellow—one of the best—but you can't get away from the fact that he insists on spending most of his life in this rather mouldy spot."

"Is it mouldy?"

"Pretty mouldy, from what I have seen of it. All right if you care for being buried in the country——"

"It's a pretty place. As far as I've seen—from my window."

"It *is* pretty," agreed Lord Tidmouth. "Very pretty. You might call it picturesque. Have you seen the river?"

"No."

"It lies at the bottom of the garden. Except during the winter months, when—they tell me—the garden lies at the bottom of the river."

Lottie shivered.

"It wouldn't be a very lively place in winter, would it?"

"Not compared with some such spot as London."

"Are you living in London now, Squiffy?"

Lord Tidmouth nodded.

"Yes," he said, "I've come back to lay my old bones in the metrop.—when I've done with them, that's to say. I've got a rather sweetish little flat in the Albany."

"The Albany!" breathed Lottie wistfully.

"Right in the centre of things and handy for the theatres, opera houses, and places of amusement. All the liveliest joints within a mere biscuit-throw."

"Yes."

"Wasted on me, of course, because I never throw biscuits," said Lord Tidmouth. "You must come and see my little nest."

"I will."

"Do."

"Have you plenty of room there?"

"Eh? Oh, yes, lots of room."

Lottie paused.

"Room for me?"

"Oh, yes."

"I mean—what's the word I want?"

"I don't know, old thing. Where did you see it last?"

"Permanently," said Lottie. "That's it." She came to him and grasped the lapels of his coat. She looked up at him invitingly. "How would you like to have me running round the place, Squiffy?"

Lord Tidmouth wrinkled his forehead.

"I don't think I'm quite getting this," he said. "It seems to be sort of floating past me. If it wasn't for the fact that you're so keen on Bill, I should say you were——"

"I'm going to give Bill up."

"No, really?"

"Yes. I couldn't stick it here. The old boy was quite right. It would give me the willies in a week."

"Something in that."

"And the thought crossed my mind——"

"Well?"

"It just occurred to me as a passing idea——"

"What?"

"Well, you and me——"

"What about us?"

Lottie pulled at his coat.

"We always suited each other, Squiffy," she said. "I'm not denying we had our rows, but we're older now, and I think we should hit it off. We both like the same things. I think we should be awfully happy if we had another try at it."

Lord Tidmouth stared at her, impressed.

"Perfectly amazing you should say that," he said. "That very same thought occurred to me the moment I saw you at Bingley. I remember saying to myself, 'Squiffy, old man,' I said, 'haven't you rather, as it were, let a dashed good thing slip from your grasp?' And I replied to myself, 'Yes, old man, I have!'"

Lottie beamed at this twin-soul.

"I'm awfully fond of you, Squiffy."

"Awfully nice of you to say so."

"After all, what are brains?"

"Quite."

"Or looks?"

"Exactly."

"Kiss me."

"Right-ho."

"Nice?"

"Fine."

"Have another?"

"Thanks!"

"Once again?"

"In one moment, old thing," said Lord Tidmouth. "We will go into this matter later, when we have a spot more privacy. I observe our genial host approaching."

He waved his hand at the last of the Bannisters, who was coming in through the french windows from the lawn.

CHAPTER XIV

BILL was peevish.

"Oh, there you are!" he said, sighting Lottie.

"Yes, here I am."

"'Morning, Bill," said Lord Tidmouth agreeably.

"Go to hell!" said Bill.

"Right-ho," said his lordship.

Bill turned to Lottie.

"Are you proposing to stay here long?" he asked.

"No," said Lottie, "I'm going off to London with my future husband."

"Your—who?"

"Me," said Lord Tidmouth.

Bill digested the news. It did not seem to relieve his gloom.

"Oh!" he said. "Well, a fat lot of use that is—now."

Lottie looked hurt.

"Bill, I believe you're cross with me."

"Cross?"

"Isn't he cross?" asked Lottie, turning to her betrothed for support.

Lord Tidmouth adjusted his monocle and surveyed Bill keenly.

"Yes," he said, having completed the inspection, "I think he's cross."

Bill quivered with righteous wrath.

"You've only ruined my life, that's all."

"Oh, don't say that, old top."

"I just met her in the garden." Bill's face twisted. "She wouldn't look at me."

"Who wouldn't?" asked Lord Tidmouth.

Bill brooded a moment. Then he turned to Lottie.

" Breakfast is ready in the morning-room," he said. " I should be much obliged if you would get yours quick—and go."

" Well, I must say you're a darned fine host!"

" Oh, get along!"

" All right," said Lottie proudly. " I'm going."

" Save the brown egg for me," said Lord Tidmouth. " I must remain here awhile and reason with this bird. Bill," he said reproachfully, as Lottie left the room, " you're very hard on that poor little girl, Bill. You show a nasty, domineering, sheiky spirit which I don't like to see."

" I could wring her neck. What did she want to come here for—and last night of all nights?"

" But be fair, old man. She was sent for. Telegrams were dispatched."

" Sent for?"

" Yes. By the aged relative. He wired to her to come."

Bill stared.

" My uncle did?"

" Yes."

" Why on earth?"

" Well, it was like this——"

Bill blazed into fury.

" I'd like to wring his neck. Where is he? I'll go and have a heart-to-heart talk with the old fool. What the devil does he mean by it? *I'll* talk to him."

Lord Tidmouth followed him to the door.

" Steady, old man. Be judicious. Exercise discretion."

He realized that his audience had walked out on him and was now beyond earshot. He came back into the room, and was debating within himself whether

108

it were best to breakfast now or to postpone the feast till after one or two of the murders which seemed imminent had taken place, when Sally came in from the garden.

"Oh, hullo!" he said. "So you got here?"

"Yes," said Sally shortly.

"Well—er—good morning and so forth."

"Good morning."

Lord Tidmouth may not have been one of the world's great thinkers, but he could put two and two together. This female, he reasoned, had turned up, after all, last night, and had presumably seen instantly through poor old Bill's pretence of illness. This would account, in his opinion, for her air of pronounced shirtiness.

"Nice day," he said, for want of a better remark.

"Is it?"

"If you're looking for Bill," said Lord Tidmouth perseveringly, "he's gone out to murder his uncle."

"I am not looking for Mr. Bannister."

"Oh!" said Lord Tidmouth. "Oh? Well, in that case, right-ho. Coming in to breakfast?"

"No."

"Oh!"

There was a silence. Lord Tidmouth was not equal to breaking it. Conversationally he had shot his bolt.

It was Sally who finally spoke.

"Lord Tidmouth."

"On the spot."

Sally choked.

"That woman. . . . That—that woman. . . . How long has she been here?"

"Lottie?" said Lord Tidmouth.

"I don't know her name."

"Well, it's Lottie," he assured her. "Short for Charlotte, I believe. Though you never know."

"Has she been living here?"

"Absolutely not. She arrived last night, round about midnight."

"What! Is that true?"

"Oh, rather. The old uncle sent for her."

"Sir Hugo? Sir *Hugo* sent for her?"

"That's right."

"But why?"

"Well, as far as I could follow him, it was something to do with psychology and all that sort of rot."

"I don't understand you."

"Well, it was this way. I gather that he thought old Bill was pining for her, and he fancied it would cure him if he saw her in the old ancestral home. Old Bill had nothing to do with it. He got the shock of his life when he saw her."

Sally drew a deep breath.

"Oh, well, that's a relief."

"Glad you're pleased," said Lord Tidmouth politely.

"I thought my patient had had a relapse, which, after I had been working on him for three weeks, would have been too bad."

Lord Tidmouth was seeing deeper and deeper into this business every moment.

"Old Bill's potty about you," he said.

"Indeed?"

"Absolutely potty. Many's the time he's raved about you to me. He says he could howl like a dog."

"Really?"

"And, as for Lottie, if that's the trouble, don't give her another thought. If it's of any interest, she's going to marry *me*."

Sally was surprised.

"You? But that's very rapid, isn't it?"

"Rapid?"

"I mean, you've only seen her about twice, haven't you?"

Lord Tidmouth laughed indulgently.

"My dear old soul," he said, "the above and self were man and wife for years and years and years. . . . Well, at least eighteen months. I am speaking now of some time ago, when I was in my prime."

"You mean you used to be married to—her?"

"Absolutely. And we've decided to give it another try. You never know but what these things will take better a second time. I think we'll be like the paper on the wall. Great Lovers of History, if you know what I mean. I can honestly say I've never married a woman I felt more pally towards than Lottie."

Sally held out her hand.

"I hope you'll be very happy, Lord Tidmouth," she said.

"Thanks," said his lordship. "Thanks frightfully. And you?"

"What do you mean?"

"Well, my dear old thing, I mean, now that you know that Bill's relations with Lottie were strictly on the up-and-up, and realizing, as you must do, that he's perfectly goofy about you, what I'm driving at is, why don't you marry the poor old blighter and put him out of his misery?"

"Lord Tidmouth, mind your own business."

Lord Tidmouth winced beneath the harsh words.

"I say," he said plaintively, "you needn't bite a fellow's head off like that."

Sally laughed.

"Poor Lord Tidmouth! I oughtn't to have snubbed you, ought I?"

"Don't apologize. I'm used to it. My third wife was a great snubber."

"I was only annoyed for a moment that you should think I could possibly be in love with Mr. Bannister."

Lord Tidmouth could not follow this.

"Don't see why you shouldn't be," he said. "Bill's an excellent chap."

"A rich waster."

"Handsome——"

"Mere conventional good looks."

"Kind to animals."

"Well, I'm not an animal. If ever I fall in love, Lord Tidmouth, it will be with someone who is some use in the world. Mr. Bannister is not my sort. If he had ever done one decent stroke of work in his life——"

"You're pretty strong on work, aren't you?"

"It's my gospel. A man who doesn't work is simply an excrescence on the social fabric."

Lord Tidmouth's monocle fell from its resting-place.

"Pardon me while I wince once more," he said. "That one found a chink in the Tidmouth armour."

"Oh, you!" said Sally, smiling. "One doesn't expect you to work. You're a mere butterfly."

"Pardon me, I may be a butterfly, but I am not mere."

"You're not a bad sort, anyway."

"Dear lady, your words are as music to my ears. Exit rapidly before you change your mind. Teuf-teuf!" said Lord Tidmouth, disappearing in the direction of the breakfast-room.

Sir Hugo came bustling in from the garden. A recent glance at his watch, taken in conjunction with a sense of emptiness, had told him that it was time he breakfasted.

At the sight of Sally he stopped, astonished.

CHAPTER XV

HE peered at her, blinking. He seemed to be wondering whether much anxiety of mind had affected his eyesight.

" Doctor Smith!"

" Good morning, Sir Hugo."

" I had no notion you were here."

" I was sent for—last night—professionally."

" Somebody ill?"

" Not now."

" Are you making a long stay?"

" No. I shall leave almost immediately. I have to be in London for my hospital rounds."

" Oh! Have you seen my nephew William?"

" Not since last night. Lord Tidmouth says he went out to look for you."

" I am most anxious to find him. I have something of the most vital importance to say to him."

" Yes?" said Sally indifferently.

" I am endeavouring to save him from making a ghastly blunder and ruining his whole life. He is on the very verge of taking a step which can only result in the most terrible disaster. . . . By the way, I knew there was something I wanted to ask you. When you putt, which leg do you rest the weight on?"

" I always putt off the left leg."

" Indeed? Now that's most interesting. The left, eh?"

" Yes."

" Some people say the right."

" Yes, J. H. Taylor says the right."

" Still, Walter Hagen prefers the left."

" He ought to know."

" Yes. I remember seeing Walter Hagen hole a most remarkable putt. He was fully thirty feet from the hole on an undulating green. He——" Sir Hugo broke off. Something with the general aspect of a thunder-cloud had loomed through the french windows. " Ah, William," he said, " I was looking for you."

Bill gazed at him blackly.

" Oh, you were?" he said. " Well, I was looking for *you*. What's all this that Tidmouth tells me?"

" Tidmouth tells you?"

" Yes, Tidmouth tells me."

" Tidmouth tells you?"

A spasm shook Bill.

" Will you stop that cross-talk stuff!" he cried. " What Tidmouth told me was that you had got hold of some asinine idea that I'm in love with Lottie Higginbotham."

" Quite correct. And what I say, William, and I say this very seriously——"

Bill cut in on his oration.

" There's only one woman in the world that I love, or ever shall love," he said, " and that's Sally."

" Sally?" said Sir Hugo, blinking.

" I'm Sally," said Sally.

Sir Hugo looked from one to the other. He seemed stunned.

" You love this girl?" he gasped at length.

" Yes."

Sir Hugo raised both hands, like a minor prophet blessing the people. His mauve face was lit up with a happiness which as a rule was only to be found there on the rare occasions when he laid an approach-putt dead.

" My dear boy!" he boomed. " My dear young

lady! This is the most wonderful news I have ever had. Bless you! Bless you! My dear doctor, take him! Take him, I say, and may he be as happy as I should be in his place. I'll leave you. Naturally you wish to be alone. Dear me, this is splendid news. William, you have made me a very happy man. What did you say your handicap was, my dear?"

"Six—at Garden City."

"Six—at Garden City! Wonderful! What the Bannisters need," said Sir Hugo, "is a golfer like you in the family."

He toddled off, rejoicing, to his breakfast.

CHAPTER XVI

BILL laughed nervously.

"I'm afraid," he said, "Uncle was a little premature."

"A little, perhaps."

"But don't you think——"

"No, I'm afraid not."

"I had nothing to do with Lottie being there last night."

"I know that."

"And doesn't it make any difference?"

"No."

"But, Sally——"

"No. I'm afraid you're not my sort of man."

"I love you."

"Is love everything?"

"Yes."

"No," said Sally. "Respect matters, too."

"I see. You despise me?"

"Not despise. But I can't take you seriously."

"I see."

She thought that he was going to say more, but he stopped there. He walked to the desk and sat down.

"I'm sorry," said Sally.

"Don't mention it," said Bill coldly. "Have you had breakfast?"

"Not yet."

"You'd better go along and have it then. It's in the morning-room."

"Aren't you having any?"

"I had a cup of coffee just now in the kitchen. I don't want any more."

"Have I spoiled your appetite?" asked Sally demurely.

"Not at all," said Bill with dignity. "I very seldom eat much breakfast."

"Nor do I. A very healthy plan."

Bill had opened the drawer of the desk and was pulling papers out of it. He spoke without looking up, and his tone was frigid.

"You will excuse me, won't you?" he said formally.

Sally was curious.

"What are you doing?"

"I thought of doing a little work."

Sally gasped.

"Work!" she cried, astounded.

She drew a step nearer, her eyes round.

"Yes," said Bill aloofly, "business connected with the estates. I've been neglecting it."

"Work?" said Sally in a whisper.

Bill regarded her coldly.

"You won't think me rude? I've got rather behind-hand. I've been a little worried lately."

"I didn't know you ever did any work!"

"Oh? Well, I do—a considerable amount of work. Do you suppose a place like this runs itself?"

"But I never dreamed of this," said Sally, still in the same hushed voice. "Do you mind if I sit here? I won't disturb you."

"Please do," said Bill indifferently.

She settled herself in a chair and sat watching him. Ostentatiously ignoring her presence, he started to busy himself with the papers.

Some moments passed.

"How are you getting on?" she asked.

"All right, thanks."

"I won't disturb you."

"That's all right."

There was another silence.

"You don't mind my sitting here?" said Sally.

"Not at all."

"Just go on as if I were not here."

"Very well."

"I would hate to feel I was disturbing you."

"Kind of you."

"So I won't say another word."

"All right."

There was a brief interval of silence. Then Sally got up and stood behind him.

"What are you working at?" she asked.

Bill looked up and answered distantly.

"Well, if the information conveys anything to you, I am writing out an order for some new Alpha separators."

"Alpha—what?"

"Separators. They are machines you use to separate the cream from the milk."

"How interesting." She came closer. "Why do you want Alpha separators?"

"Because I happen to own a dairy-farm."

"You do? Tell me more."

"More what?"

"More about your dairy-farm."

Bill raised his eyebrows.

"Why? Does it interest you?"

"Tremendously," said Sally. "Anything to do with work interests me. . . . An Alpha separator; it sounds complicated."

"Why?"

"Well, it does."

"It isn't. If you're really interested——"

"Oh, I am."

Bill's manner lost something of its frigidity. His dairy-farm was very near to his heart. He had fussed over it for years, as if it had been a baby sister, and he welcomed the chance of holding forth on the subject. So few people ever allowed him to do so.

"It's based on centrifugal force," he said.

"Yes?"

"Here's a diagram." An ardent note came into his voice. "That thing there is the reservoir."

"I see."

"Below it," proceeded Bill emotionally, "is the regulator with a float-valve——"

"Go on," said Sally, thrilled.

All the coldness had now left Bill Bannister's demeanour and speech. An almost fanatical note had replaced it. He spoke with a loving warmth which would have excited the respectful envy of the author of the Song of Solomon.

"As soon as the regulator is full," he said, his eyes shining with a strange light, "the float-valve shuts off the influx."

Sally was all enthusiasm.

"How frightfully clever of it!"

"Shall I tell you something?" said Bill, growing still more ardent.

"Do!"

"That machine," said Bill devoutly, "can separate two thousand seven hundred and twenty-four quarts of milk in an hour!"

Sally closed her eyes ecstatically.

"Two thousand——"

"Seven hundred and twenty-four."

They looked at one another in silence.

"It's the most wonderful thing I ever heard," whispered Sally.

Bill beamed.

"I thought you'd be pleased."

"Oh, I *am*!" She pointed. "And what's that little ninctobinkus?"

"That——" Bill paused, the better to prepare her for the big news. "That," he said passionately, "is the Holstein butter-churner."

"O-o-oh!" breathed Sally.

He looked at her anxiously.

"Is anything the matter?"

"No, no. Go on talking."

"About milk?"

Sally nodded.

"Yes," she said. "I never knew it could be so exciting. Do you get your milk from contented cows?"

"They've never complained to me yet," said Bill. He placed his finger on the paper. "See that thing? The sterilizer!"

"Wonderful," said Sally.

"That's the boiler there. At seventy degrees centigrade the obligatory and optional bacteria are destroyed."

"Serve them right!" said Sally. She looked at him with almost uncontrollable excitement.

"Do you mean seriously to tell me," she asked, "that you are familiar with the bacteria of milk?"

"Of course I am."

Sally's eyes danced delightedly.

"But this is extraordinary!" she cried. "The *Cavillus acidi lactici*——"

"The *Bacillus lactis acidi*——"

"The *Bactorium koli*——"

"The *Bacillus erogenes*——"

"The *Protens vulgaris*——"

" The *Streptococci*——"

" The *Colosiridium butiricum*——"

" The *Bacillus butiricus*," cried Bill, rolling the words round his tongue in an ecstasy. " The *Bacillus sluorovenus. And* the *Penicilium glaucum*!"

Sally leaned on the desk. She felt weak.

" Great heavens!"

" What's the matter?"

" It can't be possible!"

" What?"

" That you actually do know something about something after all," said Sally, staring at him. " You do do work—decent, honest, respectable work!"

The fanatic milk-gleam died out of Bill's eyes. Her words had reminded him that this was no congenial crony who stood before him, but the girl who had flouted his deepest feelings; who had laughed and mocked at his protestations of love; who had told him in so many words that he was not a person to be taken seriously.

He stiffened. His manner took on a cold hostility once more.

" I do," he said. " And from now on I'm going to work harder than ever. Don't you imagine," he went on, his eyes stony and forbidding, " that, just because you've turned me down, I'm going to sit moaning and fussing over my broken heart. I'm going to *work*, and not think about you any more."

Sally beamed.

" That's the stuff!"

" I shall forget you."

" Fine!"

" Completely."

" Splendid!"

" Put you right out of my mind for ever."

" Magnificent!"

Bill thumped the desk with a ham-like fist.

" As soon as you have left this house," he said, " I shall order new tractors."

" Yes, do," said Sally.

" New harrows," said Bill remorselessly.

" Bravo!"

" And fertilizers."

Sally's eyes were shining.

" Fertilizers, too!"

" Also," thundered Bill, " Chili saltpetre and Thomas tap-cinders."

" *Not* Thomas tap-cinders!"

" Yes, Thomas tap-cinders," said Bill uncompromisingly.

" I never heard anything so absolutely glorious in my life," said Sally.

The telephone bell rang sharply. Bill took up the receiver.

" Hullo? This is Mr. Bannister. . . . For you," he said, handing her the instrument.

Sally sat on the desk.

" Hello?" she said. " Yes, speaking. . . . Now. . . . Quite impossible, I'm afraid. . . . You might try Dr. Borstal. He substitutes for me. . . . I can't possibly leave here now. . . . The case I am attending to is very serious—much more serious than I thought. . . . Good-bye."

The interruption had caused another radical alteration in Bill Bannister's feelings. Forgotten were the stout-hearted words of a moment ago. Looking hungrily at Sally, as she sat swinging her feet from the desk, he melted again. Forget her? Put her right out of his mind? He couldn't do it in a million years.

" Sally!" he cried.

She had jumped off the desk and was fumbling in her bag.

" One moment," she said. " I'm looking for my thermometer."

" Are you feverish?"

" That's just what I want to find out."

" Sally!"

" Go on," she said, " I'm listening."

She put the thermometer in her mouth. Bill stood over her, though every instinct urged him to grovel on the floor. He was desperate now. The thought that soon she would be gone—right out of his life— lent him an unusual eloquence. Words poured from him like ashes from a Thomas tap-cinder.

" Sally . . . Sally . . . Sally . . . I love you! I know you're sick of hearing me say it, but I can't help myself. I love you. I love you!"

Sally nodded encouragingly.

" M'm," she said.

" I never knew how much I loved you till I saw you here—among my things—sitting on my desk. Won't you marry me, Sally? Think of all the fun we'd have. You would love this place. We would ride every morning through the fields, with the clean, fresh wind blowing in our faces."

" M'm."

" And all around us there would be life and move- ment . . . things growing . . . human beings like carved statues against the morning sky. . . . The good smell of the earth. . . . Animals. . . . Ben- zine and crude oil. . . . Benzine and crude oil. Sally!"

" M'm!"

" It's summer. The fields would be like gold in the

morning. Sparkling in the sun. Harvest-time. Ripe wheat. Do you hear, Sally? Ripe wheat shining in the summer sun, and you and I riding together. . . . Oh, Sally!"

She drew the thermometer from her mouth.

" I have no fever," she said.

" Sally!"

" But I'm trembling, and my pulse is a hundred and ten. And—do you know——"

" What?"

" I've lost control of my vascular motors."

" Sally!"

" One moment. I am faced with the most difficult diagnosis of my career. I ascertain the following: the organs are intact. I have no pain, no fever; but the pulse is a hundred and ten. The reflexes are heightened. On the periphery of the skin I note a strong radiation of warmth. A slight twitching in the nape of the neck. The hands tremble. The heart action is quickened. Every symptom points to something serious—something very serious indeed."

" You're ill."

" I'm not ill. I'm in love. Yes, that is what I diagnose: acute love!"

She looked at him.

" Do you remember what I said to you that day we met? If I ever found a man I could love I would tell him so as frankly as if I were saying good morning."

She came towards him, holding out her hands.

" Good morning, Bill!"

" I say," said Lord Tidmouth, manifesting himself suddenly in the doorway, " do you two know that breakfast——" He broke off. His educated eyes, trained by years of marrying one woman after another with scarcely a breathing-space in between, had taken in the situation at a glance. "Sorry!" he said. "Excuse it, please!"

The door closed. From the passage beyond they heard his voice announcing that he feared no foe in shining armour.